MAURIA

Steve North

BFE PRESS
LOS ANGELES, CA

This book is a work of fiction. Names, characters, places and incidents either are the product of the author's imagination or are used fictiously, and any resemblance to actual people, living or dead, business establishments, events, or locales is entirely coincidental.

Published by BFE Press
Los Angeles, California
www.brookforestentertainment.com

Thanks to Joey Green, numerous friends whose suggestions improved *Mauria*, and the mountains of Colorado that sent this story through me.

Cover photograph and interior photographs © 2010 by Steve North
Author photograph © 2010 by David Carlson
Book design by Joey Green
PRINTED IN THE UNITED STATES OF AMERICA

Library of Congress Control Number 2010917481

ISBN: 0983126178
ISBN-13: 978-0-9831261-7-1

10 9 8 7 6 5 4 3 2 1

For my wife Barb
and my daughter Dustianne

PART ONE:
"Winter"
YearMauria 1208

CHAPTER ONE
'Winter Love'

Blisfur had love-bitten Kurk. He had grabbed his arm in fright, watching her orange-tinted saliva soak into the tiny wound. He had reached for his alloy reed, its shiny knife-edge menacing the smiling Blisfur. He felt the warm ooze of drug enter his mind. He became too weak to even wave the alloy knife. He rolled about in the Carpetweed, feeling the cool bristles tickle his face. An Orclid pod puffed under his chin, his jaw twitched, and his teeth snapped into an apple fruit which had rolled against his mouth.

A liquid warmth spread from the bite on his arm to his shoulders, his foot twitched and then surrendered to the cascading river of colored sensations.

He smiled.

He laughed.

Blisfur had come upon him. Her bites sent further ecstatic waves of tingle through his body and then they were deep in the throes of Mating.

A strange sight indeed—Kurk's bulky, white body entwined in the many splashes of bright color-hair upon Blisfur's Vuerven, thin form, her blue forehair dancing over Kurk's cliff-like forehead. Her yellow and blue waisthair skirting under him and smoothing the ground beneath his white, shaking mid-section.

And yet, these two contrasting shapes swayed in ecstatic oneness, . . . her chirp-like cries of glee and his deeper Maurian moans danced lightly on the breeze.

For Kurk, no time passed. All of time passed. For Blisfur, she felt her new Circle.

Later, they lay in helpless afterglow through the night.

The new Sun kissed them awake.

Kurk's first thought was . . . "How could this have happened?" It came back to him. He had wandered from his queue of brightly clad hunters. His meandering, brush-crackling steps had stumbled upon a lush Vuerve. She was an incredible blue and yellow flag in the spring greenery. She was flowing animal! Something had given way within him, he stared at her and tried to picture her reduced to garnished strips of meat on some MisterSir's dinner plate.

For of all the Maurian Heroics, Kurk found hunting the least palatable. His Integrity had once come under question from this very idiosyncrasy—his lack of lust for the hunting kill. "Quirk," his associates at MarPrex chided Kurk. But the other branches of Maurian endeavor allowed for some peculiarities in MarPrex Heroes. After all, Populous Relations demanded a different bent than MarSek's army and security, or MarSupply's food marketing, or even LifeCo's reproduction futures.

"Creative" Heroes were viewed as a necessary evil, anyso. It took a special breed to take information and news, then twist and turn and invent only that which would inspire images of Maurian success and Integrity. Not anyone could bail out the real Heroes when things went awry; could metamorphosize disasters into triumphs; could push on straight ahead, regardless of the cost—this was the "creative" challenge. This was Kurk.

For the soul of Mauria was to move from here to there, no matter what. It was MarPrex which would clean up afterwards.

But the part of Kurk which conjured creative concepts at MarPrex couldn't get along with the Mr. Kurk who sought Heroism hunting afield. They were as different as he and this Vuerve.

Thus, as he had aimed the shiny SonaGun to his prey, his fingers faulted at the trigger. The dart that should streak from the SonaGun, and slay this pleasant creature—readying her for the KillRacks, the slaughtering, the processing—that deadly projectile remained in the chamber. Because at that very instant, Kurk would have rather eaten Grell for a year than kill this colorful creature of the hills and valleys. Not only was she amazing in her colors, her stance, but there was something . . . somehow sad and even lost about her form and face.

And Blisfur had heard Kurk, and wondered of his not shooting her. She was, as Vuervee became, at End—a place on the Circle which awaited Sign and rebirth, so the next Circle journey could begin. Ganfer, her own Mate of many changes, and leader of all Vuervee, had Ended with a Maurian dart. She was the new VeemVa, but too sad to guide. And so, she sought her Circle, her Sign, and wandered dangerously amid the foothills near Mauria.

And it—or *he*—had come, this Maurian hunter! But he did not shoot? What did this mean? She had Mented to his approaching form, but could not understand his frightened face.

He had stumbled closer to her.

"I am Kurk," he had stammered.

"I am Blisfur. Why do you not shoot your dart?"

"I don't know."

"Am I too old to eat?" she urged.

"You are . . . too sad to eat."

"I have lost a Mate. To one of your hunters. The Circle is. What have *you* lost?"

"My . . . courage, it would seem. What is the circle?"

They had not understood each other. But by LateSun, they had learned of each other in the most shocking way possible.

Mating was a dour, petty crime in Mauria. But Mating with an animal . . . a Vuerve—table fare . . . !

Such things were only whispered about, or hinted at after too many SourDrinks.

But so, and yet it had happened, everso.

Kurk would report in day next, telling of catching his foot in a crag; of breaking his Corder and being unable to call for help. Blisfur had found her strange and unexplainable Sign, and would move on to lead all of her children and theirs—her Veem, the Veem of Blisfur—with love.

CHAPTER TWO
'Reflections in the Ice'

Blisfur, a Vuerve, and Kurk, a Maurian, were in love.

Now in YearMauria 1216, eight of Kurk's full seasons later, they sat as they had quite often, upon the same host of CarpetWeed, on the same ridge they had first come together. Some of the blue-gray and orange growth lie dormant under forming ice.

"What is a Hero?" asked Blisfur.

"What all Maurians seek to be," answered Kurk, smiling at her Vuerven innocence—that he had come to love.

Kurk rolled his tunic collar to the many rolls of his old chin, in response to an ever chilling wind. About them the EdgeHill forest stood its quiet sleep of strength against the cold, the wind. Steam rose from the metallic alloy of Kurk's CO_2 belt and tube, which clamped to his nose. Despite these obstacles, Blisfur loved his proud Maurian features, so opposite to her kind.

His soot-black eyes sought hers of blue. They tunneled from the caverns of his white, loose cheeks. His pulpy, high-bluffed face profiled against her Vuerven slimness, which age had made sharp and sinewy. A decorated, metallic ForeBar sat over Kurk's brow, covering his forehead. His Maurian black hair allowed no hues or reflections.

"Are you a Hero?" asked Blisfur, her clear deep eyes reflecting the impish beauty of her form. Even in old age, her skin retained an auburn, muscular glow. Her colorhair had faded little. She had blue-green headhair which tickled her shoulder. She had sun-yellow forehair above her eyes which washed her proud face with a bright glow.

Her waisthair, brittle-thin from many changes, fell from waist to knee with wiry brown warmth. A webwork of tendons undulated as she toed designs in the crusty snow.

"I would be," said Kurk, "the lowest form of criminal if my people knew of us. Hardly a Hero, my Lady! The Heroes in CityMauria would be duly upset that I don't **hunt** you. But to *talk* to you, to . . . uh . . . "

"Mate with me?" perked Blisfur.

"Yes, as we have done . . . . this is cause for *more* than the WorkHouse! It is an impossible loss to Maurian Integrity. Not for me, everso; but we are the first ever to speak, to touch, to . . . "

"Love?"

"If you say."

Kurk's harsh, Maurian baritone and Blisfur's soft Vuerven chirp danced about the quiet setting, strange partners indeed.

How much had changed since Kurk's errant hunting chapter so long ago.

The icy wind, which this day tore at deep caverns of warmth in the last recesses of the body; was then a flower breeze, cradling the ever-sweet smells of Cartha and Jimber and Coyotia upon its gentle arms. Ripe, crimson bushberries and apple fruits of endless varieties and sweetness lie about the ground or hung swollen for the choosing.

And Kurk had been in his prime, and Blisfur had been of new ripeness. But such was not true today, eight Winter's later.

This was a day for both to feel their age, their stoic decay, their enveloping indifference. Indifference also lay upon the dim Winter-green of the Needletrees as harsh gusts whipped between hissing branchlets dropping brittle, unfeeling cones and withered seed pods. Blisfur and Kurk sought indifference, too, from the twisted happiness of their love.

For any Vuerve might lose the Circle to see a Maurian hunter and Vuerven friend together such as this.

None in CityMauria knew of them. His metallic city lay many of Kurk's Unimeters to the east, down and past the face of the Edgehills, on a flat and symmetrical grid on the Plains.

And none of Blisfur's Veem of Vuervee, many of her valleys and skies towards the setting Sun, knew of them.

And yet they were.

"Who could have believed," said Kurk on this day so many ages later, "that we could have young together. What are their names again? Say them."

"Dillon, Venes, Hiola. Some think they are the second brood of Ganfer and I. I have not told them of us."

"Your names still sound ugly to me, after all this time."

"Time?"

"Uh, . . .changes?" helped Kurk.

"Yes. You are getting fat, like all the other Maurians."

"I am a Maurian. And I am not fat. You are skinny, unnourished."

"My colorhair brittles. I am coming to my End and my beginning."

"When you die, you die."

Kurk's tiny eyes squinted into a new gust of snow-sprinkled wind. His classic Maurian lips—thick, red upper and slim, pink lower—grimaced.

"We are both to End soon," said Blisfur.

"Yes. I . . . want to see them."

"You cannot. You would frighten my Veem. And our young. If a single Vuerve saw their leader with a Maurian, they would . . . "

"Yes, tell me about the Vuervee again."

"You do not Ment to them. You cannot."

"Tell me," he pleaded.

"We live. We are. We run from your hunters. We begin and End with the Circle, and begin again. You live by the line. We know not of it. You kill—to kill another is to kill yourself."

"I won't be angered! It's the Vuervee who are primitive! You are unable to consummate a simple SonaLine. It is the basis for all Sonology."

"You have told me this."

"We shall always dispute. You can't see the benefits, can you? Why, I could speak to you from *Mauria*—with you up here in the mountains—just in this little Corder."

"Of what good is this?"

"We could . . . *speak.*"

"We are speaking. You could not touch me."

"You could at least keep yourselves warm in Winter, with our alloy tunics?"

"I am cold because of age. That is when to End and to begin."

"Grell! Girl Grell! I could make you live many more Winters."

"We already live more seasons than you. What is Grell?"

"I . . . nothing important," Kurk said.

"It is to do with us. You will tell me."

"It's too . . . hard to say."

"There is no hiding of the mind!"

"Well, aah, I've told you. In Mauria, we keep things inside our heads. You know?"

"I have asked you. You will tell me what this Grell is," she said and her eyes bore into his like a shaft of Sun through Cone trees.

"Grell is . . . chopped . . . meat," Kurk stammered quickly, softly.

"Chopped Vuerve. Dear Circle."

Blisfur's face broke into tears, quaking her frail old form.

"I cannot bear tears. Please, stop it," Kurk said, looking away, as if Maurian troops might come over the hill and rescue him from this crying, this ultimate loss of Integrity. He stammered and bloated on, desperately trying to stop the tears.

"There is none else *to* eat! If lesser animals than you roamed about . . . "

"But for the Maurians, there would be. We still know of the

winged and furry beings your people Ended. But for your ways, you would breathe the air as we. It is passed on that your people even Mated for young . . . long ago."

"Never!" Kurk shouted.

"You could eat the plants, as we do."

"We cannot! Anymore than we could sit around staring at the mountains and the sky like you do without . . . *doing* something to better, to advance, to discover new secrets. We have paid our price for that, and have answered our challenge and restored our Integrity."

"What means pay . . . price?"

"It is not important. I love you, not your anim—people. The Vuervee choose to live like beasts, and are treated . . . "

"That is cruel to say. We live by the Circle. Its ways unfold to us. We cannot escape its movement, even so. So we learn from it and teach ourselves to spin with the Circle."

"All is *not* smooth, "Kurk interrupted, snapping. "It is <u>us</u> who cure the diseases of your food, it is *our* machines which plant enough seeds so that more of your young can live."

"So there are more for you to hunt," Blisfur sighed.

"We have kept you and us alive!" he proclaimed, "and these tubes we breathe into are our medals of Heroism, our war wounds! And we wear them proudly!"

Blisfur understood little of this last statement, but saw that Kurk had crested and then kneeled in sadness from it. She looked upon this Maurian, and felt her heart.

"I love you, Kurk," she said softly.

"Don't you understand? I know we've made mistakes, but most Vuervee, including *you*, wouldn't even be here were it not for *our* medicine, *our* machines, our control programs, *our* . . . uh . . . "

"Your hunger?" Blisfur finished. "But we *are* here, Kurk. I *am* here. And you love me."

Kurk heaved a great sigh.

"Yes. I love you, . . . my Lady. Everso."

"Everso, my . . . Hero."

Kurk smiled at the Maurian word.

"I . . . unghh!"

Kurk had whipped his head to his knees. Great grunting and hissing noises came from his bubbling lips. He fell to the crusty snow. Blisfur jumped for his tube, which dangled loose. She clamped it into his nose, and he turned the small wheel on the CO_2 cylinder attached to his belt.

"You are indeed near End," Blisfur laughed, "why did you keep your tube away from your nose?"

"I've . . . I somehow hoped I could adjust . . . in small doses to more Oxygen."

"Occsee . . . "

"The air up here."

"You should not come here if you can only breathe in your city."

"But for you."

"But for me, I have a hard climb to my Veem. I will begin. I will see you on the early Sun after the next snow, if the Circle allows. I love you. I am you. Have care of your form."

"Goodbye, my Lady."

* * * * * * * * * * * * * *

Kurk rejoined his snowprints in reverse, and began the traipse to Mauria, whose shiny gray-walled outline rose from the flatland below the rim of the first Edgehill. A late Sun cast a pink tinge over the snow. A hard, light blue sky reflected the bitter cold.

Had Kurk not been diverted, he might have reached Mauria by middle night, but a hoarse cry from the North pinned his attention. He stumbled to a slow ridge tangled with dwarfed Whitebark trees and gazed through his scope.

There, on the very next uplift of land was a blue and orange tuniced hunter. A fellow Maurian. The lead Hero of a Winter hunting queue. The hunter also peered through his scope, and Kurk panned his own in the direction the Maurian was scanning. What he saw made him drop his own viewer in the snow, as well as his whole utility belt.

Blisfur!

He had to take large hops across the snow, for it had piled deep during a robust Winter. He calculated a point whereby he might intercept him before the hunter approached near enough to get a shot at her.

Blisfur, a small flash of color in the distance, was climbing a rock pile, humming a tune, unaware.

The icy air soon made the CO_2 cylinder pour freezing air into his straining lungs. Under his metal tunic, his body was a slick of sweat. His heart began to panic, for if Blisfur should lie dead on this cold-hearted day . . .

He emerged from a dip, and saw the Maurian taking bead on her.

She was such an easy target as she struggled up a short bluff that Kurk simply plunged down into the snow, hiding his eyes from view of his lover's death.

But as the icecrust burnt his face, he suddenly perked his head. No. No. No. . . . Yes!

The Maurian hunter was still adjusting the long range viewer on his gun. The Hero would undoubtedly take luxurious time in lining up such an unwary old target.

Kurk's SonaGun blared its high-pitched squeel as it rocketed a triangle formation of darts. It took the small alloy darts a fraction of a moment to leap across the canyon between them. The hunter looked up quizzically as the cylinders silently punctured his tunic. Then, suddenly his right arm twitched straight to the sky, his feet took three sprinting steps, and he plunged over the rocky cliff. Two orange tunics peered from the valley below. They ran to the dead

man. They looked around. They spotted Kurk, standing with his gun still aimed.

Blisfur looked far below her, and scurried over the rockmantle, her frail legs at high pitch towards her Veem. The Veem of Blisfur.

Kurk fired another volley over their heads, and began stumbling to the West—away from Mauria.

Kurk of MarPrex, CityMauria, was now a dead man.

The Hunters would report, and MarSek would be waiting at his return. He had killed an Integritorial Maurian! In Mauria, one could be sent to the WorkHouse for *crying*, much less murder! Now tears of a lifetime froze on his chin, and still he cried. Some Hero!

And still he trudged.

He had to plod the long way around the rockbluff which Blisfur had scaled. By the time he found her prints in the snow, it was dark. He shone his light onto the CO_2 cylinder . . . enough left to make it to his Lady before death. Soon his legs worked by themselves, uncommanded by his mind which flickered scenes of Mauria to his frosted eyes.

Though he was now the Maurian misfit of all time, he would miss his gray metal city. His alloy, railed, symmetrical city, where scores of FareBeams intercepted hundreds of others in perfect cross-hatch. SonoRails would now carry thousands of Maurians to their places of work.

His Mauria. He hated it. And he loved it. It was a magnificent monument to reasoning. It was clean. The furnaces, the massive Sonology in constant motion, the endless filtering, production, waste disposal—for all of that, dear Mauria it was clean! It survived, it succeeded. It won.

And now, without him.

He pushed on, following her snowprints.

He brushed under a needlebough. Just below, two Vuervee were finishing a splash in a steamy hot spring. He waited. Watching the antics of these two colorful animals set a great loneliness to him.

The steam against the cold cast a dreamy tone; and Kurk's sad eyes drifted from the ice-framed, steamy water to the twinkle of stars above tall jagged peaks to the West.

He could see a number of—what had Blisfur told him?—oh, yes, "wombs," in the quarter moonlight. They were huts woven of branches.

The young Vuervee leaped from the water's warmth and ran to a nearby womb, where they burst into the portal, laughing and screaming. His Maurian Integrity revolted at such uncontrolled behavior, such expression of primitive emotion.

But within him, something reached out for its strange warmth, its innocence. I am to die now, he thought. I am a disgrace to the Maurians, I am unlike these animals. A soft vision came to him, hidden in the mist of the rising steam. A blue Vuerve reached out to him with a Circle in his hand. Kurk thought he saw himself reaching out to this blue animal with a long pole. But more likely, he thought, his CO_2 was running low and he was hallucinating. Best to move on fast.

It was to a clump of three wombs set near the river that Blisfur's tracks blended with a host of others. He crept as silently as was Maurianly possible to the first one. Inside, a Vuerve held still, having heard Kurk the moment he stepped on the hard-pack snow which surrounded the Vuerven Veem of Blisfur. Others had heard and did the same. They all listened, and waited, and clutched BirthGems around their necks for hope. To kill another is to kill yourself, they repeated silently to themselves.

To kill another is to kill yourself. This was a tenet that all Vuervee held as bond, and that which protected them from the hunter even as they were hunted.

There were, however, two Vuervee who did not hear the obvious noises from Kurk's approach. The womb of the VeemVa, Blisfur, was the oldest shelter of them all. Within this cavernous hut her son Tedrin, and Blisfur writhed upon a soft mound of leaves. They were Menting, in a trance, touching minds and thoughts. As they hugged and felt

each other's soul for Sign, for path, for sensing what will be, the effort made them groan and twist about, deep into the other's thoughts.

Just outside, Kurk heard this slow and quiet moaning. It sounded like Blisfur. A short, deadly "pfft" came from his tube, as the last life-giving CO_2 filled his lungs.

This was it, he had only moments to live. And from the groans within, Kurk believed that Blisfur was dying, too. Perhaps the Maurian Hunters had fired a dart after all. How fitting, he thought. How perfect. Their love would end as one, together at last . . . forever! He would hold her, and he would die with her.

Kurk staggered into the womb, not caring about noise at last. Two dark forms moaned and heaved on a bed of leaves. He flicked the light on his CompBox, hoping he had not missed Blisfur's last moments. Give me this, at least. A Hero's last moment with his Lady . . .

Tedrin leaped up from atop Blisfur's aged and wispy form. They were still heaving with fast breaths, both covered with sweat. This is the final joke, thought Kurk! Loving this . . . this animal has brought me to this supreme mocking of my Integrity! Lady, indeed! Vulgar *animal*! Mating at her age! I save her life . . . she repays me by . . . I'll kill her! I'll do what I should have the first moment I spotted her!

Kurk's Oxygen-poisoned eyes darted from old Blisfur to her son, Tedrin, to a brood of three very young Vuervee on the floor.

His children?

A blind rage pulsed from stomach to neck, and a purely Maurian revenge erupted. Killing was too easy. Maurian CounterFlow taught resistance to primitive reactions like rage. I'll die like a true Maurian . . . with Integrity! Everso.

She doesn't know, Kurk plotted. She doesn't know my cylinder is empty. I will make her live with my death as if she did it!

Kurk dramatically ripped his tube from his nose and flung it before Blisfur.

"To kill another is to kill yourself?" he spat. "You have killed me now!"

Kurk burst outside and headed for the warmspring.

He heard Blisfur shriek "No!" from a corner of his mind.

He leaped into the water. It was radiantly warm, and soon replaced the tortuous Oxygen in his lungs. By the time the current carried him under the ice, into the freezing water downstream, Mr. Kurk, 14th ViceCouncillor of MarPrex, was dead.

CHAPTER THREE
'Blisfur's Seeds'

The Sun fell low casting a mysterious, changing glow on the mountains and valleys of the Vuervee. In great contrast, CityMauria was bathed in a cool and pink late Sun which uniformly reflected off this metal island of perfectly executed rails and structures, its square plot covering only that part of the flat plains to which it had chosen to claim. The borders were clear and clean.

A veiled mushroom of atmosphere hung over the city, the never sleeping furnaces.

There was no random chance here, no sprawl, no haphazard activity. CityMauria was exactly what it was planned to be. What a perfect habitat for a race who viewed the world as an uncomfortable, disorderly place in its natural state—messy, unpredictable—and who were guided by an overpowering urge to tidy, to control, to arrange.

Integrity.

The Maurians.

Aggressive shapers of their own destiny, they were experts at reaping the fruits of technological manipulation; superb at catching human instinct before it became action. And then: isolate it, observe, experiment, process, classify. Next: decide whether or not it fit in with the plans. If not: change it, reverse it or modify it as per goals.

Integrity.

The Maurians.

Don't flounder like the Vuerven animals, letting Nature push you about as a twig down a stream, change it!

Integrity.

Don't let genetic flaws run rampant through the generations, control it. Let LifeCo inject Ladies with pure Maurian Extract which could be controlled and altered to bring out the best. Let MarPrex follow behind, convincing every Maurian that Mating was for animals and criminals . . . like the Vuervee.

Make these children of LifeCo the high Mr. Sirs, the leaders. For they were pure, and their physical mutations were certainly not deformities, but rather the mark of the New Maurian perfection.

Turning back was never a possibility, not for Maurians—and especially not for the New Maurians . . . who were now in charge.

And so, by this YearMauria 1200's, Mauria had used its science to deliver and isolate itself from the cruel, askance forces of the harsh world outside.

It bred its own Heroes, it breathed its own air.

And best of all, its food supply was no longer dependent on the disgusting disarray of stupid, disease-carrying and sometimes dangerous crawling and flying things which used to roam about before the New Maurians had risen. Eating such lowly life forms couldn't have a good effect on a Mr. Sir's Integrity, everso.

No, Mauria had genetically created a herd of intelligent and unviolent creatures to hunt and fatten itself upon, the Vuervee. Every Maurian could be a Hero on the hunt. Every Mr. Sir's Lady could dine on fresh, Prime Vuervee. Everyday.

Mauria was precisely where it wanted to be.

* * * * * * * * * * * * * * * *

Tedrin stared from the weeping Blisfur to Kurk's discarded tube lying on the floor, as steam from the hotspring enveloped the Vuerven Veem, and the dusk changed to winter's night.

The half-moon of red in Tedrin's otherwise brown head and forehair hung over his deep, sad frown of bewilderment.

He had been near the river. The steam had made him see a vision of his Ended father, Ganfer. This vision of Ganfer seemed to point urgently towards his mother's hut. When he had crawled into Blisfur's Womb his Mother had beckoned to him.

But his eyes were drawn to the three sleeping young, Dillon, Hiola and Venes. An aura danced above them, yet Tedrin could not feel Ganfer's Circle about them. Why could he not Ment to Ganfer in this youngest brood?

Were they not of Blisfur and Ganfer, as was he?

"Come to me," Blisfur had said. "You will learn of the broken Circle."

"A Circle cannot be broken . . . " Tedrin had begun, but then approached his Mother, Blisfur, and lay upon her to learn.

Mother and son had Mented deeply, until both felt Ganfer's vision. The power of this vision, this truth, had made both of them sweat and writhe and pant. At the height of this Menting, a light had swept the womb and a Maurian with crazed eyes—angry—threw his tube upon the floor and ran off to die.

Now, in the calm of the night, Tedrin asked to know of it.

"My son," Blisfur began. Tedrin cried at how old and withered she was. "This Maurian was a Sign. You must hear. This Maurian friend . . . he and I have . . . we have known Mating, together. He must have thought you and I were Mating."

"No," said Tedrin. "This is not so. You, my mother, Va of all Vuervee, Mating to a Maurian?! There is no such Circle . . . "

"You must hear. For you will soon guide the Vuervee on a path around this Circle."

"This is not a path," sulked Tedrin, "no Circle can . . . "

"You would want a clear path through this life, I know. The Circle hides its truth until the journey is done, and you are back at the beginning. Want you a rutted, straight path such as the Maurian hunters use? For such clear lines, trees must fall and flowers must die."

"But to love a Maurian . . . "

"You love all things. We love all that is." A pain shot through Blisfur's chest. "Your Circle, Tedrin, begins and ends with this Maurian, so listen close. Look to these sleeping young, my son," she pointed to Dillon, Hiola and Venes asleep on the floor. "These were not of Ganfer and I—as you and Sereoul and Colia were. They were of loving Kurk. The Maurian."

"My Circle twists at such a thought! There can be no . . . "

"My son. You will carry this knowledge with you, the truth within the seed."

Blisfur's pains were worsening, but the vision gained strength.

"Many many changes from now, you will get a Sign. And you will know it is time to tell of this. *Tell it to Dillon, or Hiola, or Venes. And you will know which to tell—for one of them will enter this same Womb as did Kurk on another day of great confusion for you, the new Veemva.* The Veem of Tedrin."

Tedrin bowed his head. He had never thought to be VeemVa. His younger brother, Sereoul, had more love of guiding. His sister, Colia, had the great and calm strength of body and mind. But he, Tedrin, unsure of step, . . . to be Va? . . .

Blisfur's continued vision interrupted his thought.

"Yes, oh, yes, Tedrin. You will protect this seed of change to its End and beginning. Sereoul and Colia. They will weary of this valley, the Maurians. They will take others like them away from here. My pain, . . . my son. Comfort me."

Tedrin, with the enveloping calm of his destiny warming his sadness, gently held his Mother's hand and stroked the forehair above her dimming eyes. The young forms of Blisfur's last brood— Dillon, Hiola and Venes—remained in deep sleep through it all, branch-slitted moonlight falling across them. Hiola stirred once.

Blisfur continued, her eye on a snowy peak which could be seen through a hole in the womb branches.

"It is yours to see this Circle through, which has happened here, dear Tedrin. I know not why. The Circle stopped Kurk from shooting his gun. We . . . spoke . . . . we loved. It is all for good. It is all for you to help finish, all, even the Maurians are in the Circle."

"But the Maurians are of the line, Blis . . . "

"All is of all. A line is but a Circle partly hidden from our view."

Blisfur painfully stood up, clutching her chest. She smiled, and walked lightly out of the womb, never leaving her eyes from the peak high to the West.

Blisfur, mate of Ended Ganfer, mate of Ended Maurian Kurk; left the Veem of Blisfur on this night and it became the Veem of Tedrin.

She paused at the side of the warmspring.

She gently pushed Kurk's CO_2 tube into the soft ground so that it stood.

She hugged Tedrin one last time. He cried.

Then she began her climb to the peak which was shown to her. She would End and begin on this tall peak, and she would be carried through the canyons in very late Spring indeed!

The Circle is.

She walked and climbed and the snow gathered on her hair. As she struggled over the ice-formed rockcrest atop, she broke the thin vine which held her Birthgem around her neck. The small, round gem had been sealed the day she began her life's journey around the Circle.

She cracked it open on a jagged rock point. A handful of bluish Mindo seeds fell into her frost covered hand. The pains had stopped. She was warm and sleepy.

Smiling, laughing, she walked in a slow arc, dropping a seed here and there. Beneath the ice on her aged body, a flowing warmth glowed and covered her inside and out.

She lay down.

Her form was soon wind-covered of gentle snow, as were the seeds she had left.

PART TWO:
"Spring"
YearMauria 1241

CHAPTER FOUR
'Cold Sun'

Dusk settled its flat gray upon the land, filling valleys with black and sending an eerie tint upon the Plains. As the Sun's faltering glow, now but a vague rim-light behind the mountains to the West, turned a cold red, it was difficult to discern between the gray metal relief of CityMauria and the darkened flatlands from which it sprung.

A dim cloak of cool mourned the warm bright day of early Spring that had been, which lay in the shadowed remnants of cold dayset.

This was a heartless time of day which made one forget the Sun's warmth so soon before; which shook one's feeling that Spring was on its way. But Spring, like anything else, was inevitable, as was growth and change.

And in this YearMauria 1241, some thirty-three after Kurk's indescretions with Blisfur, the only human life on Earth had, indeed, grown and changed on this island of dry land in a world covered mostly by ocean.

Instead of one Veem of Vuervee to hunt, the Veem of Tedrin, the Maurians now had three. True to Blisfur's vision, Tedrin's sister Colia had taken many young, stout Vuervee far North to the edge of the Table Mountains. There they stood boldly with her against the bitter cold, where Maurian hunting queues rarely bothered the tundra, and found a Circle of survival to turn upon.

Tedrin's brother, Sereoul, had done likewise. But Sereoul, whose multi-colored head, fore and waisthair were a sight to behold, chose the South for his Veem; where soft mountains and rolling desert burned with vegetation colors to match his own.

Yes, life was spreading and branching to new forms, despite the crises and the mistakes. Nature was, indeed, forgiving.

But even *She* was fascinated with Dillon, Hiola and Venes, young of the Maurian Kurk and the Vuerve Blisfur.

****

His blue eyes searched. His blue colorhair trailed a breeze. His slim legs folded beneath, as he rested upon moss rock. The purple starburst chutes of Tenatorna plants clumped around his lookout.

From this EdgeHill, Dillon gazed down to Mauria.

To kill another is to kill yourself, he murmured silently. To hate another is to hate yourself.

Yes, metallic Mauria, below on the Plains, often brought icy hatred to his soul. How was it he Mented to feelings no other Vuerve could think of? What fruit was this?

Would that he could love the Maurian hunter as the soft flower breeze that now tickled his tanned skin. That he could love the hunters as he loved the great Circle, as all other Vuervee did.

He had seen the question in many Vuerven eyes, but they accepted him as they lived the Circle; and accepted the Maurians. And so they embraced the turbulent Dillon, son of Blisfur.

Dillon searched for signs of hunting party. Bobber, Duerr's mate of Winter last, was to bear young, and was not quickly moved. Dragna, Dillon's own Mate, had also been so when she fell to a Maurian FieldDay. She had been a proud blue Vuerve, like Dillon, but with bright green forehair.

He had watched from the arms of a tall, saving Needletree, as she flinched and kicked from the darts, as she tried to crawl from brightly dressed hunters. She was carted off on decorated pageant. He had heard them cry, "A kill with young!" They were very excited.

His young. *His* mate. Food for the bloated hunters, . . . the Maurians.

As Dillon Mented to this earlier day, his wiry hands became taut from squeezing a dew-marked rock. His anger grew.

He thought of the Circle of the Vuervee, . . . the line of the Maurians.

The moss peeled and slipped beneath his angry, scratching fingers. He Mented long to these tiny slicks of green. And Dillon found a Sign of the Circle in the simple rock moss; whose tiny green clovers continued their beauty and life, beside those which had been rended by Dillon's clawing anger.

A breeze blew across the EdgeHills with promise of larger Sun, and happy, warm days ahead. He jumped to a higher bluff, letting his form hang by his arms. He felt his back tingle from new blood. He grabbed a crag with his hand and hoisted over the edge.

A laughing formation of wind-smooth red rock laid before him. Dillon's blazing blue forehair and waisthair, and muscle-rippled skin formed a quivering statue against the cakey-smooth rocks.

A clumsy rustling of undergrowth bade him to look below. There, beyond a Whitebark stand, three Maurians puffed and heaved, carrying a pageant through a hunting trail. Four Ended Vuervee sprawled from the pageant's alloy poles.

Surely not all Vuervee could weather the agony which ripped Dillon's soul from this view? The anger! The hate. But he knew other Vuervee could, and that he could not, even as this could not be!

To hate another is to hate yourself . . . to kill another is to kill yourself.

Dillon saw the shiny colors of hunting tunic hung carefully on a tree. Now the Maurians rolled their sleeves. One withdrew a small reed, which soon sprung magically into a large one, its blade flickering star-shaped reflections in the Sun.

The blade rose and fell, and rose and fell more times. Then the heads of four Vuervee lay on the ground.

"To kill another is to kill yourself," Dillon spoke aloud.

Soon red and purple innards joined the gruesome pile below the pageant. Dillon felt the Parsnian leaves of his early meal rumble in his gut. He swallowed hard.

These, Dillon knew, were wrong-doers, even for Maurians. Vuerven kill were promised of long ago to be carried whole from the mountains.

The Maurians were very strange, thought Dillon, and he began to cry.

* * * * * * * * * * * * * *

In CityMauria the workday staled, and many a Maurian Hero counted the time till closing. A stagnant wig of synthetic atmosphere shrouded Mauria from long days burning of CO_2 furnaces.

In the Mountains, the Vuervee of the Veem of Tedrin prepared wombs for the icy night of new Spring certain to be. Evenso, some made walks and climbs, free of worry for Maurian hunters, who never sported past early dusk, preferring the walls of their city on the Plains. Hunting in the hills for tender Vuervee was just fine when one could see, and not freeze.

In these hills, Tedrin gathered the more aged Vuervee in thicker wombs, in piles for warmth. Their brittle fore and waisthair could not stay the cold from thin bodies of many changes.

Considerable Maurian UniMeters to the North, where the stunted icehill tables guarded sparsely vegetated lowlands, and the Sun twinkled from far away—even in summer—Tedrin's sister Colia awoke from winter sleep to chop snow and ice from the portal of the food cave. Her Veem had been asleep since middle Winter.

Many Ranges to the South Tedrin and Colia's brother, Sereoul, led a learning walk in the waning light. Spring had visited his Veem some time ago, and a world of dark and bright plants were already in growing.

But in CityMauria, at InterFares 27E-45N, a different kind of survival was going on.

* * * * * * * * * * * * * *

Small gamer and ParlorMan Bordt scanned his near-empty gaming room and cursed. Only one customer stalked the low-cost artifacts in the rear, a series of metal clicks echoed with his steps. This was not an unusual sound in CityMauria since everything from boot to building, tunic to table, was fashioned from metal alloy— in this case, old and unbuffered alloy; its musty, unpleasant odor clinging to the counters and walls.

Unless things pick up a bit, it'll be Grell for awhile, Bordt stewed. Less and less anyso, one saw high Mr. Sirs seeking the recreation of small gaming.

The last one was that—what was his name—oh, yes, Curn. Mr. Sir Curn of MarSek. Mr. Sir braggart, Bordt remembered, for the man had shoved his tutillage right in Bordt's face. Within moments, this Curn let it be known that he was born of top Maurian B-10 Extract, that his father was a high Mr. Sir in Family Industries, and that this musty little gaming parlor was well below his standing.

"And what may ye' pleasantries be on this fine day?" Bordt had asked with admirable CounterFlow, since he would have much rather put a dart between the man's pompous eyes.

Mr. Sir Curn had chosen a game of Terrain, being in MarSek himself, Mauria's military and security force. A great Hero, was he, in MarSek.

But not on *that* day. No. Within a short time, Curn was begging Bordt for just one more game, at top BookCredits. The old mirror piece reverse! The so-called Integrity of these high Mr. Sirs sometimes made them see through their feet! Ho ho. He had eaten prime Vuerve for a month of that!

But . . . things had slowly degenerated all through the gaming district. Probably just a cycle. If those Grellheads at Family Industries . . .

Bordt clumped his elbows and sinewy hands on the counter, placing his head upon this cradle of boredom. He glanced out the window to the FareWay. The FareBeam, thick as a Maurian waist, glistened in its bisection of this metal highway. The hundreds of

SonaRails that slid on this beam each day had rubbed a bright sheen into the alloy.

Bordt was an ugly man. It depended not on how he dressed, or how he combed his thinning and fading black hair, or which fashion of ForeBar he chose to span his pocked forehead, or even which EnFirm Gell he applied to his warty, mottled face. His head was both long and thin and fat. His ugliness seemed to focus at the tip of his nose, where it bulbed upward.

Were he a Mr., or a Mr. Sir, the cosmetic technology would be available. He was ugly as a child, too; smart in school, but ugly Maurians were always tested to unfeasible extremes. True, it wasn't all cruelty. Professors knew an ugly man's chance of using what he learned in school was as barren as the dusty Plains around CityMauria.

So a commoner he was. But an owner, too. And that made for something. The gaming boards, machines, and number games which heaped his Parlor mimed the garrish deceptiveness of his features.

For many an Integritorial Hero had sought easy mark in Bordt's clever clutter, only to be gamed right out of their expensive tunics by the ugly man in his ugly shop.

Bordt watched a short, intent commoner man pumping BookCredit after BookCredit into a number game at the store's rear. Small Book. Bordt only blinked once in the next while, when the whoosh of the ForceVent just to the side of his shop spewed its 200 cubic units of CO_2 into the air. Those cursed ducts.

If his shop was in a Family Industries District, you better sure believe they would install the new SonaVents! How's a small ParlorMan supposed to make Book when his walkway trade is scared half to death every 4Time on the mark? And now, what with those shiny young Family Industries executives taking training shifts at the FI shops, their Parlors were open all the day and night, everyday of the year!

But . . . there was still a *feel* to the old small gaming Parlors which kept the more clever ones in trade. Bordt's was one of these.

CHAPTER FIVE
'Early Sun'

It was 300 in the morning.

Larl's RecParlor swelled with a feisty crowd of Misters. The broad red stripes of the Family Industries Insignia hung on walls of patterned alloy. SourDrinks chuted from a forest of hands. The Misters grumbled a wave of small talk, prior to heading out for work.

Mr. Larl, a tall goblet-faced man with small oval eyes, considered the day's trade from his office alcove high above. Nothing wrong with a packed Parlor of Misters, nothing indeed! The largest crowd rimmed a hot game of Terrain, which noisily unfolded in a corner. Terrain was the forte of all Maurians. It was the reverse of most board games, and outsold them by piles. There were two parts to the game: Disarray, and array. The first step found each contender placing the opponent's pieces in disorder, far away from the latter's home squares. The final goal was to move one's pieces, which slid or leaped in various modes, backwards towards the beginning, or home squares. It was a game of chaos to order, shambles to Integrity, commoner to Hero.

CityMauria itself was the ultimate Terrain game; an arranged place of home-square living and breathing in a world otherwise unsupportive of Maurian life.

Near the serving counter, an innocuous man paid Credits from his Book, gulped a last draw of his MindoSour, and left. His name was Mr. Granes, and you might say his most notable feature was how well he fit into the crowd.

Outside, Mr. Granes emerged from Larl's into the steamy FareWay. The burning dizziness of his last toke of SourDrink pulsed in his limbs. He rambled on the walk towards his parked SonaRail.

Mr. Granes was 54th ViceCouncillor of LifeCo, the Reproduction Control division of Family Industries. He was slightly thin by Maurian standards, though possessed enormous cheeks for his size. His deep black Maurian eyes seemed threatened by encroachment from the massive cheek-puffs. In contrast to high, loose cheeks and jowls, his forehead was set at a deep angle back. His black hair, which all but a few Maurians boasted, swirled over a small balding spot atop his bluff-like head.

Granes' SonaRail slipped down the FareBeam in mechanical dance. He headed for InterFares 87N-22E; the location of MarPrex's Populous Relations building. Mr. Sir Burn, Councillor of LifeCo had sent Granes an exciting communique . . .

> Granes:
>
> New chart at MarPrex. Check it out and report.
>
> —Mr. Sir Burn

Granes felt his Integrity swell for being chosen to do this.

Back at LifeCo's section of scientists, Granes was in charge of a small clique of level-3 executives. Their job was to execute level-3 estimates of Reproduction Schedule Quotas. In simple terms, Mr. Granes' office would submit quotas suggesting how many new Maurians could be produced, based on projected food supply for the Vuervee and a plethora of environmental data.

There were twenty-seven other such offices which performed this same function. The quotas would be averaged, and then adjusted by the high Heroes of LifeCo in accordance with classified data.

Mr. Granes' SonaRail swerved onto a SideFare which led into the bowels of MarPrex's office structure. Like almost every building in Mauria, this was of gray alloy, perfectly square, and with standard

Maurian letterset on the alcove. It read, "MarPrex . . . A Section of Family Industries," just as Granes' SonaRail read, "LifeCo . . . A Section of Family Industries."

Before Granes exited the scoop door of his parked vehicle, he grabbed his CompBox and dialed the LifeCo band. He was rewarded with a bright, chipper commentator.

"Thank you for tuning in, Heroes," rasped a voice, "The current population resource of Integritorial Mauria is: 8 Mr. Sirs, 12,880 Misters, 10,464 CommonerMales, 426 Ladies, and 2,165 CommonerFemales. Hunter's report an approximate resource of 3,872 Vuervee. Last unit's kill of 1,234 has been refilled by new Vuerven births as of two days past at 970Time. Hunting quotas are up .35 to 2.75 Vuervee-per-Group. The current . . . "

Thus informed, Mr. Sir Granes hopped the lift to Mr. Sir Fruke's alcoves. Amidst the metallic screech of the lift, Granes tensed for CounterFlow.

CounterFlow, that exciting process of Integrity! It was a cloak, like his tunic. CounterFlow reversed instinct, that morbid substance which promoted emotion, expression, and a glob of other disgusting low-level responses. CounterFlow would cloak his nervousness at coming face to face with the high Councillor of MarPrex, Mr. Sir Fruke, head of all Populous Relations!

Emotions!. Everso, what was the point of life if one could not unshackle oneself from horrors like sadness, irrationality, and—yes—even Mating.

Mr. Granes remembered his own indiscretion too clearly. It had been a CommonerGirl whom he had caught stealing. As he had struck her time and again, he began to hold, and even rub across her semi-conscious form. And then he . . . well, it mattered not. He had had her whisked away to the WorkHouse, where she'd probably chop Grell for the rest of her days, anyso.

In Fruke's preroom, a squat CommonerMale with off-brown eyes took Granes' name and politely thrust his head into the high

Hero's alcove. Mr. Sir Fruke's booming voice acknowledged Granes' presence, purposely carrying to where Granes sat.

"Excellent!" the Councillor of MarPrex rumbled from out of view, "any Hero who understands all that scientific stuff is welcome here!"

From his seat, Granes felt the glow of importance. The CommonerMale at the appointment desk didn't seem as impressed, suggesting this is nothing new, but managed a somewhat deprecating tilt of a smile to Granes.

Mr. Sir Fruke burst through the portal and stepped quickly to Granes. Granes had never seen anyone so gigantic.

"Yes! Yes, how *are* you Mr. Granes! My, LifeCo certainly knows which of its Heroes will create a big impression! Yes!"

"Well," stammered Granes, cheeks aflush, "I've . . . uh, always . . . uh . . . "

"Come right in! Come right in! Say, that tunic of yours has a marvelous cut to it! Where did you buy it?"

"Hrmnn, over at . . . "

"Say! The chart is right in here! Have a look!" Granes gulped and followed the immense Councillor into a side alcove. Grell!, he cursed. His CounterFlow had stayed in the lift! He felt like a silly schoolboy again. You would think he was in the presence of the great SilverForm Wigged leader of all Mauria, Mr. Sir Councillor Blench!

"I *know*," continued Fruke, "that your own Hero at LifeCo, Mr. Sir Burn, will be en*thralled* at this little dolly work! Hah! When these charts replace the old ones all over CityMauria, I'll Book you complaints drop by half! Yessir! Half!"

The chart was lit brightly by hidden spotbeams, and purported to graphically chart the votes and power of the Control Council which ruled all of Mauria with Mr. Sir Councillor Blench at the helm.

As Granes cleared his head enough to study the chart, he finally spotted the masterful situation traverse which lay within. This chart would have us believing there were eight votes, with Councillor

Blench having two—LifeCo, MarPrex, MarSek, EnvirCo, Family Industries and MarSupply each with one. Fair enough.

However, the Councillor of Mauria was also the Councillor of Family Industries, which controlled LifeCo, MarPrex and MarSupply.

Thus, Blench really had *five* votes out of eight! A joke? A joke, indeed. But for this: Nothing . . . *nothing* was what it seemed in CityMauria.

Let's suppose, for example, that Mr. Engineer Rute of EnvirCo and Mr. Sir Fruke of MarPrex had a power-coup in mind. Unlikely, but then again if a Mr. without a Sir before his name—as in Mr. Engineer Rute—had dreams of being the first Councillor of Mauria from the unrespected sciences, he might need quite a powerful Mr. *Sir* in legion with him. Say, a Mr. Sir who controlled something as devastating as the media—as in MarPrex, as in Mr. Sir Fruke, who might push a Mr. Rute into the office of the SilverForm Wig in return for being next in line.

If we suppose all of this unlikely nonsense, then we might further suppose that this chart, soon posted in every public FareWay and structure in Mauria, had another edge to its reed—unseen by Councillor Blench, current ruler of all Maurians. Blench would be so grateful the chart camouflaged his dictatorial power that he may not hear the hidden bootsteps.

Let us suppose that those bootsteps, that second edge of the blade, was nothing more than putting the name of Mr. Engineer Rute *visually* close to the office of the SilverForm Wig on the chart, with a "Sir" slipped in. *You* know, so people could start getting used to the idea of an engineer in high respect.

If that sounded a bit confusing, consider the fact that all across CityMauria, other plans and strategies were also in motion. It was part of the natural scenery in CityMauria.

Even Mr. Granes saw it, as he took the lift to street level, the new chart tucked under his arm. Even Granes, who was no genius, wondered if Rute was trying to ride Fruke's PR to successorship. But why and how, and who had what on whom?

Perhaps, even as we speculate on all these possibilities, Mr. Sir Fruke was dialing Mr. Sir Councillor Blench's complex at 1N-1W.

$$* * * * * * * * * * * * * * * *$$

If the lofty, patterned alloy of the Councillor's complex at 1N-1W was the height of Maurian architecture and Heroism, surely the plain, rusted walls of the WorkHouse reflected it's dimmest.

The WorkHouse was where the meat was processed.

The WorkHouse was where you were sent if you got caught stealing or killing. Even petty Mating could get you here.

Young Trebel stood shivering under the cascading water in the large showering room. She scrubbed her thin form as fast as she could, with a darting eye on the portal. Most of the other CommonerGirls in CityMauria's WorkHouse cleaned late in the day; a long, dirty day of preparing Vuerven meat.

Each day brought the same. 200Time of trimming fat from endless Primes (not that *she'd* ever get a taste), then 200Time shoving mounds of unPrime into the eternally starving mouths of the Grell-choppers, followed by another 200Time of arm-killing packing.

If the smell didn't break you, the lack of sleep would.

And yet for Trebel, the showers were the worst part. It was where the others would get a close view of her skinny form, without the bulky work tunic's camouflage. They would point, they would laugh, some would even hurt her with slaps and kicks. It seemed that no amount of Grell—or Prime Vuerve, she supposed—could fatten her up to normal for Maurians, whose stature was often measured by breadth. Even the less plump, royal Maurian Ladies turned in disgust at her animal boniness.

Her father, whoever he was, must have bought her Extract at a waste mill.

Almost done . . . just another scrub under the arms.

The showering room was also where, if she wasn't completely

precise in her positioning, she might wash out the BlackForm Dye, revealing the hidous green lock of hair just above her ear on one side. This horrible patch of Vuerve-like color hair marked her for endless humiliation until she smarted up and started covering with dye.

As Trebel shook off the water, and stepped toward the changing room, the portal opened.

She started at the imposing figure of a WorkGuard. She didn't recognize him. Her arms tried to cover her nakedness, and she turned to the side.

"Mr. Corrector Steen says you like a little . . . play," the man said, a smirk punctuating his gravelly voice, his large black eyes sweeping across like an oily towel.

"Please let me out to the changing room, Hero."

"Hero, eh?" The pre-respected title only made the Guard pause for a moment before sealing the portal. "Mating's what got ye' in the WorkHouse to start, maybe it'll be what gets you out, eh?"

Trebel let a sigh escape her shivering lips. She turned to the guard with a sadful hate, dropping her arms.

He grinned and stepped toward her, his alloy boots sending an odd echo to the wet metal walls.

As the WorkGuard's tunic, boots and pants clanged on the floor, as his white and sweaty form came upon her, young Trebel clung to her last slippery hope—that her friend did indeed carry the note to that trench-faced retch at LifeCo. Mr. Granes, indeed. Commoner Granes, if you asked her.

The WorkGuard's breath smelled of SourDrink.

She closed her eyes.

His weight mashed her spare buttocks painfully on the cold, metal shower floor.

* * * * * * * * * * * * * * * *

The SilverForm Wig lay in sloppy integrity over the back of a chair. Mr. Sir Councillor Blench, the most powerful Hero in the world, grabbed at his Corder with irritation. He was ready to take a long-awaited vacation from the affairs of Mauria at MarSek's recreation lodge, and—as the caller well knew—cared not for tiresome details of Populous Relations.

"Yes? . . . Yes. . . . I'm most impressed with the idea of the chart, Fruke, sounds like you've done it again. Most pleased. I'm most hurried, also, so I'll have to . . . yes, . . . I know . . . okay, what? Please make it fast. . . . Uh-huh. . . . Uh huh. . . . I see. Well I'd feel funny about *that*. . . . Do you really think we have to put that common engineer up there with, uh . . . Hmmm. I see. . . . yes, I understand. The votes. Still I . . . . Hmmm. Well, now that you mention it, it would make the whole chart more plausible. Yes. . . . Uh-huh. . . . Uh-huh. Oh, Grell, just go ahead with it, sounds like a good final touch. I'm off to relax, Fruke. Good work, good work. Goodbye."

Back atop the MarPrex Building, Fruke smiled at his now silent Corder, his ever uplifted eyes beamed an extra brightness after speaking to Blench. It is sometimes with a faint rustle, he thought, does a major wind begin. He scribbled out the directive which would have "Sir" added to Mr. Engineer Rute's name on the chart. It was now Mr. *Sir* Rute of EnvirCo. Fruke grinned. He *had* mentioned that little "Sir" addition to Blench, hadn't he? Well, Blench is off to relax. Why bother him with details?

And if Fruke was so clever, you might ask, why not PR *himself* into the CouncillorShip of Mauria? Well, because clever was expected, given, and common. But clever-diabolic, clever with CounterFlow, clever with patience—that's what was needed in the shifting, back-shooting maze of high politics in Mauria.

Let us not forget that Fruke's media had a complete ear to the real happenings in Mauria. His Terrain pieces, allowing the comparison to Mauria's most popular board game, were as follows:

DISARRAY: MarSek Councillor Mr. Sir Dunt had been padding the Vuerven kill, so that MarSupply's Councillor, Mr. Sir Bard, could boast an outrageous fiction of the real food supply, which was nothing to boast of. Therefore, turbulent times were around the bend, and whoever was at the controls . . . soon wouldn't be.

ARRAY: Help someone else inherit the big mess, such as Mr. Engineer—make that Mr. *Sir* Engineer—Rute. Then, when it was all done falling apart, when expectations were more realistic and achievable, then use the enormous power of his own MarPrex to steal the SilverForm Wig off this simple, trusting engineer's head. Simple, elegant, workable.

This was Mauria's natural selection of the fittest. The SilverForm Wig went to the strongest, everso.

Fruke caught his own reflection in the shiny alloy of his desk. He imagined the SilverForm Wig upon him. It looked very striking, almost as if he was born to wear it.

His booming laugh echoed from the steel walls. Yes, hodeho, all was well in Fruke's view of CityMauria.

And standing but one level down, in the main portico, still holding Fruke's chart, was another Maurian who was quite pleased. Yes, as more and more PR had oozed forth about Rute, Mr. Granes suspected he was graced with tall luck. For it wasn't every obscure Mr. of LifeCo who had Black Materials over the probable successor to the SilverForm Wig as he, Granes, had.

Rute was clearly in the wind, for whatever reason. When Rute made his bid, Granes would be right on his tunic tails!

Two plans . . . so workable, and only a room apart! How many more were there? Everso, before things resolve themselves in CityMauria, the tide would turn, and turn, and turn again.

CHAPTER SIX
'Middle Sun'

Seeing no other Maurians far below, Dillon glided away from the lowlands, lifting and dropping through the greening valleys and ridges of the EdgeHills; until snowpeaks poked into view. As he bounced from limb to rock to stream, his mood lightened Vuervenly and his bright blue hair flew in the playful breeze.

He found a good wet vaulting branch, and soon leapt gloriously, arcing almost to the very tops of Cuervo Needletrees.

A patch of Torna passed beneath, and he paused to rub through the purple leaves. The Torna adorned itself with reddish powder, play-cool to the touch, and the seeds were soon spread here and there as Dillon danced about the valleys.

Finally exhausted, Dillon sank to the warming ground, Curenat permeating the air. He buried his face and forehair in needle and carpet, taking deep, slow breaths; until he laughed so wide the ground cover filled his throat.

He drank from a deep, cold pool.

He cleaned his waisthair of barbs.

All is now, thought Dillon. He heard Vuerven laughter echoing from valley next. A gleefull string of vaults and climbs later, Dillon spotted the young. He removed a group of Mindo seeds from his headhair, and sprinkled them about the banks of a small wash. He smiled, thinking of the proud blue leaves Spring next would bring. The Circle is.

Dillon approached the young Vuervee, piled of each other in play. He let them go on for now or so, trying to see arm from leg.

He bounced into the pile. Within moments, the young Vuervee had Dillon totally covered and were playfully pulling his head and forehair.

They stopped all at once, watching Dillon. Their eager eyes, all young color of the rainbow, waited for Dillon to play. To jump at them.

Suddenly, Dillon leapt at their midst, his jump carrying for many shadows. Between the giggling, and the flying needles, Dillon recognized a blur of green and red. Muerna.

He knocked her feet gently from under, and held on. She bit his hand, but her young bite could only tint Dillon's form with drug.

While hanging her upside down, he tickled her wriggling, kicking form. "Ah, yes," he proclaimed, "this one comes with me. See the fresh bounce to her."

And now they rested, a radiant Sun caressing play-tired forms, a gentle breeze drying play sweat. They were in the helpless tickle of exhaustion, and dreamy smiles surfaced as the soft support of ground carpet tingled their skin.

Dillon, as tired as the rest, looked about these young Vuerven friends. Some were of enough changes to Mate and enter the Circle of Veem.

Like graceful Seroun, of Morna and Gingaer's Mating. Orange Seroun slept beneath a Cuervo. His maturing Vuerven color and build would sweep him from these young of soon.

"Who is what, now?" asked Dillon.

Conduella, of dewey-green waisthair, perky nose, and dark-blue head and forehair, looked to Dillon.

"I had a Sign," began Conduella. "Night last, I Ment while I rest upon a tall Needletree. I see all Vuervee . . . their faces. And when I place my own into this group I cannot see it, or it is like all the rest. Are we all like blades in a meadow?"

"Why did you choose that Needletree for sleep?" asked Dillon.

"It was all comfort boughs, and full, soft needles."

"From a distant peak, Conduella, could you have spotted such a tree? Within all the others? Did you not love it and see its differences only after you were close with it?"

Conduella giggled. Her smile made Dillon smile. The wind rustled a Panga bush nearby. Its olive colored spurs would soon have yellow and black striped flowers.

The young Mented to Dillon's thought. Then they stared into clear magenta eyes, and searched his forehair—a patchwork of rich, dark blue, and soft bright blue.

"Would it be fun," offered Dillon, "if all go to find something to shape? We will meet here when shadows are as tall as we are, and share our creations."

Dillon watched the group as they rushed off with excited smiles, so full of life, beaming with the new day's love.

* * * * * * * * * * * * * * *

Young Trebel stared blankly over the heap of Vuerven meat to be trimmed and packed.

The WorkHouse table she toiled upon was situated near one small window, offering a view to the West, the mountains poking up above alloy towers and walls.

CounterFlow, she thought, you'll be out of here soon. Suddenly, the prospect of going back to her commoner work of cleaning and serving seemed almost wondrous, compared to *this* Grell-hole!

Her tiredness made her sway. Her legs wavered and she struggled to remain atop their jittery base.

She must get out soon . . . no more guards pouncing on her, no more foul meat to knead through, a normal night's sleep . . .

Her head spun and, in her haze, Trebel fixed on one mountain peak, barely visible through the small window, and very far past the EdgeHills.

Colors . . . colors . . . an array of rainbow colors beamed from this peak.

Her eyes closed, she still saw this peak, but now it was large. Her mouth dropped open.

This rainbow of colors danced to the edge of a cliff, then broke into a myriad of dots . . . red, blue, purple, green . . .

These specks sailed off the peak and fluttered so slowly down, . . . down, . . . down into a dark valley.

"Free . . . at last . . . ," the words stumbled from her lolling lips. "Proud and free . . . "

The peak turned a bright blue and green.

"Wake up!" shouted the WorkGuard, shaking Trebel's shoulders. "You want to be Grell yourself?!"

He laughed heartily, for young Trebel had passed out into the pile of meat at her work table.

She snapped herself up, the wetness of the meat dripping down her face.

She gagged, then furiously swabbed at it with her hands.

The guard left, still laughing.

A tear joined the drippings on her cheek and then another.

Young Trebel wiped her face and neck dry.

Out soon . . . out soon, she had to believe.

For without that thought, there was not even a 10Time she could endure.

The note . . . surely it would be given to him . . .

* *

Tedrin's stocky form laughed and shivered from an icy spring, the water beading and sparkling from his brown waisthair. He smiled to the approaching Dillon. Tedrin's smiles for Dillon always wore an edge of down-turn. It wasn't really a frown, but more an after taste of the smile; much in the way one might delight in a Coyotia which has found life in an impossible rockside, but worry for its plight, its struggle, its future.

Only Tedrin knew fully of the Mating of Blisfur and the Maurian, Kurk, so long ago. He had watched the three young of these opposite seeds for many changes, as they now matured to full ripeness, even as Tedrin ripened into old age.

Dillon, Venes, Hiola . . . so Vuerven in form. When and how would Kurk emerge through them? What Maurian line would appear? As VeemVa, Tedrin would pass this leadership to one of them someday. Surely, no VeemVa had a more difficult choice.

Tedrin Mented. He wondered of Venes, whose many patches of mixed color hair reminded him of Tedrin's own brother, Sereoul. Only Tedrin knew of what source was Venes' stubborn pride and fascination with Maurian ways.

And Hiola. Of the three, Hiola's features most showed tracks of Maurian influence, though—again—only to Tedrin's knowing eye. The sloping forehead, hidden by bright blue fore and headhair. The thicker waist, covered with bright yellow waisthair. And Hiola was a theme of opposites, like his colorhair. Despite the Maurian shadows on his features, Hiola was more Vuerven in thought and action than most Vuervee! His Menting only accepted what Vuerven lore said. If all was beautiful, then all was beautiful, and there was not a drop of question in Hiola's staunch eyes. If one was supposed to plant Mindo seeds after a ceremony, then that was what one plants, nothing else, and it was as simple as that.

Everso, it was Dillon who seemed to wave and roil in the blowing elements of his twin heritage. As wondrous a bright blue Vuerve as could be imagined, Dillon's soul still quaked and cracked of most unVuerven turmoil. Hate and love, soft and hard, light and dark, child and aged one; all were planted in Dillon's forest. And to what fruits? . . . the Circle is.

Tedrin remembered Blisfur's last words:

"Tell it to Dillon, or Hiola, or Venes. And you will know which to tell, for one of them will enter this same womb as did Kurk, on another day of great confusion for you . . . "

His thoughts were burned away by the Sun and he turned to Dillon.

"It is a bright day, Dillon. Bobber is near her brood. Duerr is crazy with loving hope for them. After all the friends Duerr has saved, it is right for him to have his own! You have watched the city for hunters?"

"As you asked, Tedrin. Most stay within the city, as of last look. You seem . . . more than usual in your fear of Bobber and Duerr's brood."

"Perhaps because the Circle made me guide of the Veem but father to none of my own. I feel . . . more part of Duerr and Bobber's young than most. I am . . . too old for my own."

"All of the Vuervee are your children, you have the largest brood of all."

As Dillon slid away to rejoin the young Vuervee, Tedrin's neck felt a warm chill. Dillon, everso, left Tedrin with a sense of . . . storm?

* * * * * * * * * * * * * *

Dillon was of heavy mind and heart as he drifted slowly through the budding spring plants, leafing Whitebarks, and tall Needletrees.

Friendly puffs of cloud rolled overhead, though they darkened to the East. He came upon the young, who gathered about to show their creations. Sandeluer had made an intricate castle of Needletree berries and branchlets. Dillon admired the strong grace of the shape, the proud parts were a happy fantasy.

"Only when there are no more peaks to climb in the whole land, Sandeluer," said Dillon, "will your shapes be like another's!"

Dillon was rewarded with a hug, a lick, and a tickle. Her face laughed.

Brinta had fashioned a delicate web with needles. The contrast of brighter, green needles to goldish ended ones reminded Dillon of one he had done many changes ago. At first he didn't know of the sad twists among the shape; but then remembered the Ending of Cuernpia, Brinta's brother. The Maurians.

Cuernpia was only a child by all. Dillon wiped his tears on Brinta's and whispered to her, "For always is for always."

"But it is of pain, Dillon." It was a soft, lost tone.

"And of love," was all Dillon could say. "The Circle is."

Afterward, they placed the shapes behind for wanderers to find. Dillon feared for Brinta. He quietly followed her as late Sun rinsed its first pools of shadow through the forest.

Her form looked very small as she shuffled away. Dillon knew he should let her be . . . leave the Circle and Brinta to decide her path. She should find her own Sign.

Yet he could not. There was such darkness in her receding steps that Dillon decided he would follow her. Perhaps he was becoming weary of letting what will happen, . . . happen.

The Circle is, but was he not part of the Circle?

CHAPTER SEVEN
'Late Sun'

Mr. Granes felt the long day's sweat under his tunic. Sweat under alloy had nowhere to go, no way to dry. For Granes, another day at LifeCo in his shiny metal office had been, well, another day at LifeCo. He and sixty-eight other middle Mr.s in LifeCo had finished the day's duties. Files had been filed, mock emergencies had been solved. He had made application for 37 Promotions on the basis of his performance. The applications, in fact, were a *part* of the performance.

He smiled reflexively to the Commoner cleaning girl, who was looking at him oddly.

Her hesitant expression remained fixed on him.

"What is it?" Granes demanded, annoyed. "Answer me, you lowly rut. Why are you looking like that, anyso? Can't wait to reach the nearest RecParlor?"

The girl reached slowly into her soiled and rusted Tunic, retrieving a roll of thin note material.

He grabbed at it roughly. The CommonerGirl shook with fear, then scampered away, leaving her cleaning gear spread about.

But Granes was reading the note . . .

> Mr. Granes
>
> I will tell all before I will spend another day in this WorkHouse. I desire service work as before.
>
> Treb

How crude, Granes laughed. Trying to game *me* without Black Materials . . . no UniCopies . . . nothing! Her *word*?! A CommonerGirl in the WorkHouse against a Mr.?! And all that for a cleaning job? Ho!

He shook his large, back-sloping head with amused amazement.

With another chortle, he tossed the note into a waste bin.

Well, it was time to leave, anyso. He thought of the evening ahead, thirsting for relaxation. The Parlors? The gaming rooms? A bath and book adventure?

Mr. Granes left the LifeCo complex at exactly 620Time, opting for the walks, and leaving his SonaRail stored beneath the office.

The trek carried him towards the gaming district. When he had almost made InterFares 45W-124N, he spotted a favorite stop: "Bordt's exotic Gaming and Trading Parlor," read the sign.

Whatso? Small gamer Bordt always raised his day!

"You're back again," grinned Bordt, his half-toothed smile complemented the macabre composition of his junk-heaped gaming parlor. "And what's the latest from Family Industries, Mr. Granes?"

"Oh, LifeCo trends are up. The Industries continue to work for your good."

"That's a laugh," guffawed Bordt, "Small gamers are down 35% since FI went into amusements. The good! Girl Grell, the good!"

"While your figure is correct, Bordt, your conclusion is faulty. For one, we at Family Industries . . . "

Bordt clicked his ears off. Whenever these fatBook executives said "we" and "at," they were talking their own PR defecations.

" . . . the good of well-rounded consumers," he finished.

Granes looked about the parlor. An early Unicopy Corder hung against an alloy frame, its outdated size and lens garrish by this day's standards. Unicopies were the very essence of Maurian Gaming. After all, without the absolute certainty that there was only one copy of Black Materials—a Certified Unicopy—how could the holder of such a recording demand full favor or price for their return or destruction?

In CityMauria, a Hero could kill, lie, and even Mate without the punishment of death. But tamper with a Certified Unicopy—fake one, copy one, alter one—and you were dead. Well it should be, everso, that a Maurian Hero who was low enough to foul the very lifeblood of gaming, the final score and proof of Integrity competition, Unicopies, deserved worse than execution.

Much of the temptation had faded since this antique was produced. As Mr. Granes looked at it, he giggled at how easily one could have opened these old Corders and polluted the Integrity of the recording within.

On a shelf just below this, Granes fixed on a small, black alloy WeatherSensor. They were in great demand as items of decoration since production of the little pressurized gadgets had stopped.

"How may we game for that WeatherSensor, Bordt?"

Granes awaited Bordt's game, a pulse of excitement hung in the musty parlor air.

Bordt's thin lips dropped, "Eh, tell ye, true, Mr., I'm a bit out of sorts this day. Not much feelin' like gamin'. Whatso? I'll take 100Book fer it, and she's yours." Bordt sighed with disinterest.

"Really?" Granes asked, let down. But 100Book for a Certified sensor was a steal.

"She's yours. While you're pulling your Credits, Mr., I'll go fetch one to replace it."

Bordt withdrew to the back room, where he also lived, ate and slept. He retrieved another WeatherSensor from a shelf.

He wrote out a note, opened the WeatherSensor and placed the folded note inside it.

Slowly, tiredly, he slid a tiny chamber open to watch Granes. Granes is rather dull, thought Bordt. He will need time.

In the Parlor, the dawning of a new expression finally creased the LifeCo Mr.'s face. A barely discernible nod of understanding tilted the swept-back forehead of Mr. Granes.

Bordt smiled, and reemerged.

"It's a bone-pain, gettin' me down, Mr. Granes. Just don't have the same old Heroics in me, heh."

Bordt removed the original WeatherSensor from the display case, replaced it with the new one he brought out.

Bordt handed the other sensor, the one that was in the display, to Granes.

But Granes was grinning.

"Just a minute Bordt!" he exclaimed, "You're a bit too clever for your lowly good. You almost had me, there. Ho-de-hi! . . . too tired for gaming, eh?!"

"Eh, Sir?"

"Eh, Sir to *you*, Bordt! If these two sensors were the same, you wouldn't take the extra effort to change them! I'll take the one you just brought out and put in the display, . . . *not* the one you gave me from the the case."

Bordt conjured a mouth of transparent CounterFlow, though his slitty eyes were unreadable.

"But Mr. Granes, eh, I couldn't *certify* this one. It could be a fake! Without the proper tests, . . . "

What fun, reveled Granes, I broke his game!

"On next thought, Mr., let's forget the whole affair," said Bordt, stiff-lipped.

Now Granes *knew* he had Bordt. He dove in for the kill. This had been one heady day for Mr. Granes!

"Forget it eh? Now I know why you're offering a supposedly Certified Sensor for only 100Book . . . it's a fake! Then you bring out a *real* one in case I call MarSek to check your stock . . . and you're sitting like a Hero!"

Granes, light-headed with triumph, perked his head and spoke very succinctly for the Unicopy Corder he knew was whirring away, capturing the Game.

Bordt stared vacantly to the floor.

What a floppy bore is this Granes, thought Bordt.

"I am going to be *nice* to you, Bordt. Here is my 100Book. Ha! Give me that sensor, the other one, right now! Or shall I ask MarSek to . . . "

"But Mr. Sir! I can't certify this one is real, . . . I . . . "

Granes laughed at the spittle drooling down Bordt's chin, the lame attempt at flattery: Mr. *Sir*, indeed! He grabbed the other sensor from Bordt.

"I waive my right to Certification," Granes laughed. "And here, Bordt is your fake one back. Perhaps it will fool some other Grellhead! And thanks for the gaming, Bordt, it was absolutely invigorating! Here, have another 100Book as a tip. This real Sensor is worth 10Time that. It must be tough for you in this dingy parlor, what with FI taking over the better districts."

"Mr. Granes," interrupted Bordt. "There is no need to bother making a poor ParlorMan feel better. Why don't you open the WeatherSensor and read my note."

Bordt stared into Granes' furrowed eyes as he removed and read the note within . . .

MR. GRANES:

You have just chosen the worthless, fake weathersensor; paid 100book for it (did you also give me a tip?); And probably said that you'd waive your right to its certification. The sensor you switched it for—the one you had in your hands—was certified, and valued at 4,300book.

The certified unicopy of this gaming transaction, this loss of your integrity, will cost you another 800book.

THANK YOU FOR GAMING AT BORDT'S.

Granes burped an involuntary chuckle, which froze halfway out.

"Wha . . .We . . . ? You mean . . .?

The realization rinsed the triumph from Granes' eyes.

Bordt *always* watched the eyes at these times. The helplessness flooding in, the confidence flowing out, this was Bordt's moment. It was what he lived for. The surrender, the moment of vulnerability that excited him, even physically.

But Granes was not a sensual loser for Bordt . . . too dim, everso. Not enough height from which to fall.

"Yes, Mr. Granes. All that, and more. You became a little excited, was all. You should have realized I would never put my Parlor's name on a *fake* one," he said pointing to the real one now safely back in its case.

"Never mind, Bordt. Here is . . . another 800Book. I must say you have entertained me well, . . . a bit overpriced, perhaps . . . "

"I thank you for your patronage, Mr. Granes. Here is the Unicopy. Thank you, again."

Outside, Granes wondered about his Extract, and tossed the Unicopy into a waste vent.

A thoughtful frown soon iced the skin under his ForeBar. This was a good reminder, he scolded himself, . . . about being *careful*. These could be Heroic times for you, what with your little Engineer Rute on his way up. Maybe you're better to re-think that WorkHouse girl. Huh, you don't need a mouth flapping about, no matter how lowly.

What did he care if she wanted to scrub and shine living quarters, anyso?

Outside, Day63, YearMauria 1241 splashed its last sun-setting remnants across metallic buildings and FareBeams, turning them a bright red.

* * * * * * * * * * * * * *

Dillon watched silently above her. Brinta, immersed in melancholy shadow, had not looked up as she shuffled through the darkening woods. Dillon had been following her, and noticed she was not careful of exposing her silhouette this close to the city.

Now, she approached directly beneath him. Dillon giggled as he dropped before her. The purple sunset reflected in the dried tears of her noseline. She pushed a fading smile.

Her plump legs and shoulders stayed bowed of sadness.

Dillon and Brinta walked in silence until they came upon a grand lookout; the setting Sun cast a sea of color over the barren Plains. Close, the harsh gray outline of Mauria absorbed the deep, reflected hues, and its alloy burned red.

"It is that I care not for living," said Brinta, and her mouth quivered with hopelessness.

Dillon watched Brinta, her dimmish red waisthair, her bright red headhair and yellow forehair warmed deep, green eyes. Her mouth was of great feeling, its upper lip curved high—playing beneath a small upturned nose—and then swept down broadly. Her bottom lip was perfectly straight, and the flesh tipped out with the wet glistening of a ripening berry.

"You seek a Sign," Dillon said, "I am here. Your first love, Cuernpia, is Ended by the Maurian hunters. You are to the End of that Circle, . . . it begins again."

"Without Cuernpia. This feels not as the perfect place, the perfect Circle I have loved before."

"Of certain it is. All here is perfect. A tree stands where it stands because that is the place for such a tree to stand. A tree Ends so a new Circle can begin to grow."

"I know these words, Dillon. Of now, I cannot feel them."

"Maybe not of this day. But once I saw an Ended friend laying in a forest, and the air reeked of flesh. And his used form cast colorless shadows over all the green and blue. I wanted to End, too, and I was young.

"And I knew not of the Circle during that night. On day next, the form was still there; but the sun was shining in a loving sky, and Spring was full. It was the same as that day before, only *this* day I saw beginnings, not Endings, and young Vuervee bounced by. And the Circle was. It is known as waterview."

"I never learned of this," Brinta said. "What does it mean?"

"It means forever and never, and something and nothing." Dillon smiled.

"Look," he said, "say you walk to a still pond and gaze down. What do you see?"

"Myself?"

"Yes, but you might also see the sky, or bubbles, or water plants; or whatever you choose to see. But the very thing you are really looking at, the water itself, is the only thing you don't see!

"The Circle is waterview, Brinta. You can never really see it, only what it shows you."

It is of love, Dillon realized, that one received strength for giving it.

"Even the Maurians?"

"The Maurians, they . . . are," Dillon said.

"The Maurians, they hunt. They hunt us."

"All that is," Dillon pronounced shakily, "is of the Circle. And is perfect."

Brinta stared ahead at CityMauria and Dillon searched her. Her maturing waisthair hung reddish-gold, yellow forehair lay above green eyes.

Dillon glanced to the darkening sky.

A sudden pain settled on his neck, and he turned to Brinta. She had love bitten him, and already the wet dizziness pulled him down, down . . . down.

Brinta Mated to Dillon in heated tangle; the Sun below a cloud rim, the Moon a sliver.

In this dim light, auburn forms awrithe, young Brinta drew strength from Dillon and from herself. It was a twilight of desperate embrace for a pair of searching souls.

Soon, Dillon and Brinta snuggled in the soft warmth of afterglow and a kind, late Sun dried their wetness. Their forms were in shadow, their minds were within.

For much change they remained; until the first touch of chill sprinkled the air, speaking of night and warmth and food. Their eyes met, smile on smile in the draining light.

Brinta found strength first. Her limbs tickled and sparkled as she struggled and rose to knees and hands. A mild grimace accompanied this happy torture. Dillon was in arched recline, laughing as he watched.

Now she stood, her form perched in grace, and he had never seen her so peacefully proud—so beautiful. She had ripened and come of the Circle, all in one Sunset.

A small brown mark appeared under her eye, quietly and suddenly.

A delicate, uplifting of forehair was her only reaction to the alloy dart.

She reached toward Dillon with her eyes before she crumpled to the rock, unmoving . . . unbreathing. The understanding had not quite washed away her smile, and she Ended with some of each.

Yet another Maurian gun sent a projectile ricocheting above and around Dillon's still-frozen form. He gathered all his strength, and in a burst and a blink was over a rock and into the forest. He flew on dawning hate and anger, as no Vuerve had ever known. And when he had outpaced the pursuing Maurians, he paused.

And now, with blank emotion and odd expression, Dillon began quietly circling back.

Towards the hunters.

* * * * * * * * * * * * * *

There was a noise.

It was Maurian hunters stalking through a golden grove, their SonaGuns throwing sprinkles of reflections through the foliage, even in the waning light.

Now, another noise.

This was the sound of a dart shattering a rock.

Now came a rustling as a dark form, barely silhouetted, scurried nearby.

It was a Vuerve.

It was a Vuerve taunting the Maurian hunters, almost daring them! First it showed its body perched on a rock, then in a blue flash, it was gone, darts smacking into rocks, trees, plants.

Then it showed to the rear, and the Maurian hunters cursed and turned and swung their eyes and SonaGuns wildly about.

In the brushy shadows, Dillon bent and hooked saplings into the ground. As they released and snapped up randomly, the hunters were startled by noises all about them. There was an odd tinge of nervous jerkiness about the Maurians, as they aimed and thrashed.

One might have thought it a panic, except that no Maurian had anything to fear but from another Maurian. Perhaps it was just the darkening shadows, the unpredictable noises, or maybe the idea of a Vuerve which did not run.

One of the hunters had charged off alone in answer to a snapping noise.

He disappeared over a rise.

Now, there was a scream.

A Maurian scream.

The hunters froze, SonaGuns motionless. They stared up at a bright Vuerve, whose blue hair pierced the dusky shadows with a cool brilliance.

Dillon stood against the skyline of setting, burning clouds and shouted: "End to Maurians! End to Maurians!"

And slowly, Dillon lifted the dead hunter for all to see.

The hunter's eyes bulged, empty of sight. Dillon's hands still squeezed the soft white throat.

Dillon tensed, waiting for the whoosh of darts which should rip into him.

But all he heard was thrashing boots on leaf-coated ground . . . crackling bushes and snapping wood.

For the Maurians were rushing in frightened panic out of the hills towards the alloy safety of CityMauria. These hunting Heroes had even flung their SonaGuns away to hasten the speed of their flight.

Dillon dropped the hunter's body.

Now he stared at the quieting hills, he looked from peak to plain, from branch to sky.

But there was only a stillness, as the clouds shed their sunset colors, and stars claimed the sky.

CHAPTER EIGHT
'Mauria in Crisis'

Mr. Sir Blench heard the buzzing of a million ComBoxes. A deafening din. He fought his way to consciousness, and reached for the blue metallic ComBox on his night table. It can't be morning yet. Who would dare wake the Councillor of Mauria at 50Time on the first night of his vacation?

"Blench here, what in . . . "

"I'm not quite sure how to tell you this, sir. . . "

"Who is this? Tell me what?"

"This is Mr. Sir Dunt at MarSek Command Control Center, Sir.

"You fool. What are you doing there? Are the trees attacking us? Dunt, are you aware of the time? I'd . . . "

"Please, Blench, I wouldn't think of waking you for less than a disaster."

"A disaster?"

"Yes. I hope you're seated. It would appear that the Vuervee have taken the life of a hunter."

"Impossible. How have you verified this?" It was more a statement than a question.

"We've checked all the witnesses, Sir. Their testimony matches. We have the body. Strangled, Sir."

"And all that Grell about killing others means killing themselves?"

"I can't say, sir. We haven't really had any communication with the Vuervee for . . . "

"You know what this means?"

"Sir, there's a meeting in 20Time at Control Council. We'll expect you."

The Integritorial Hero of all Mauria—Councillor of Family Industries *and* Councillor of the Control Council—Mr. Sir Blench looked less than immortal at this hour.

His spray-bottled silver hair tangled in all directions, exposing the black roots beneath. His floppy face muscles hung rivulets of drooping skin. He stumbled to the WaterRoom. He cursed as the comb tangled and fought with his hair.

Next he splashed cold water about his head and applied EnFirm Gel liquid to the drooping areas of his face. As it quick-dried, he held a formmask to his features. Soon he checked results.

The hanging peninsulas of skin and cord now tightened and melded with the original young lines of his face. Not a day over prime did he look. His proud, stooped tallness reflected years of braving the political elements.

The office of the SilverForm Wig, he cursed. He hated waking up. Now he unhooked the alloy case from the wall, and extracted the SilverForm Wig itself. He placed it over his hair, fastened the underclips, and yelled into the masterbox for tunic and shoes.

And then he thought about a Vuerve killing a Maurian. Can't be. Obviously some mistake. A joke? Still the idea itself was enough to freeze one's blood. Impossible. The only being that could kill a Heroic Maurian was another Maurian.

We bred them, we created them . . . they can't turn on *us*!

He summoned CounterFlow so as to beat back the onslaught of imagination. The SilverForm Wig was a slippery thing to keep on your head under normal conditions, but now with this . . .

Lady Blench entered the portal, carrying his tunic. "My shoes!" he gruffed, "I asked for my shoes, too."

Lady Blench was indeed a beauty. And well she should have been. Over forty-five of the most beautiful and intelligent

Ladies had competed to do his bidding when he had taken the Silver office.

As were most high Ladies, Lady Blench was elegantly stout. Through his foggy early morning mind, Blench studied her streamlined construction. Like most Maurian Heroes of present day, Blench had never experienced physical contact with a female. He had to admit there were times, . . . frightening stirrings from somewhere deep within. But . . . to give in to such commoner banalities, this was not the path to Integrity. And, yes, there were many who have, in both high and low places in Mauria. Half of the Black Materials floating about for sale were of this topic, Blench chuckled. He had used a few himself, when all else failed. Yes, the SilverForm Wig was proof perfect that Blench kept his tails clean, strayed not from the grand Integritorial path to high Heroism.

Might as well he hadn't though, for all the good his son turned out! Mr. Sir Mimms, who was then Councillor of LifeCo, had personally bestowed Blench with Highest Grade 86BX Maurian Extract.

This, he was assured, added to the graceful intelligence of the first Lady Blench (deceased), could only yield a Son of Heroic proportions. His anger still simmered when he thought of what a low embarrassment his son had turned out to be.

Ahh, we haven't everything pegged yet, thought Blench! But we're working on it. Hah! We're working on it.

The new Lady Blench was displaying stirrings of her own, and well, he just might present her soon with a vial and injector. Better luck coming, as they say. Everso.

* * * * * * * * * * * * * *

The new Sun poked above the Plains, casting a warm icing on the EdgeHills.

Dillon shook, then trembled. A wave of twitches blew through his ragged being, and he rolled about the ground. He was coated with a sticky mass of tears, sweat, ground, and needle. A bulb of inky tundra hung from an ear, his waisthair tacked itself to various parts of his legs and torso.

He hissed as he breathed, then slashed his head into the ground, Torna dust spreading about.

He slammed his fist into a dwarf Whitebark. Now he was still for a moment. A trickle of water changed course from the pummelled ground carpet, and ran into his face.

The water cleared his mind. Dillon remembered: A noise . . . and then, . . . yes! A mark upon Brinta's forehair . . . such a tiny mark for Ending one's life. And then, a force . . . from inside. Caged too long . . . anger! . . . revenge! Ahhhh dear Circle! . . . Sweet, sweet Revenge! . . . Oughghg . . . kill . . . killll . . . killll!!

And kill he had, the Maurian's soft throat-skin bulging between sinewy Vuerven hands. *His* hands! Dillon was racked of sobs again. Soon he laid still, exhausted, limbs askew amid a puddle of tears and blood.

* * * * * * * * * * * * * *

The burnished-alloy walls of the Control Council's meeting chamber echoed the voices of the heads of Mauria. The rising Sun did not pierce this windowless, armoured room.

"But we haven't spoken to a Vuerve in thirty-three years!" said MarSek's Mr. Sir Dunt, offended.

Mr. Sir Councillor Blench banged his fist.

"It's time to stop chopping low grade meat here," Blench spat. "It's my Wig being gamed for! You're all drooling around and about, trying to dodge the heat! Figure you'll come out of your SonaRails when I'm dead and gone, eh? Listen to my lips, Heroes . . . If I go down from this, so will all of you!

"If we let this panic continue, hunting is over. The rumors are rampant! . . . Every Grellhead in every RecParlor is spinning black tales of monster Vuervee gathering to attack Mauria! I have one report that people are hoarding meat, . . . stuffing it in SonaVents to preserve it!

"You're *all* on the block for letting this jump the FareBeam while I was on my way back here! A convenient crisis to steal my Wig, you think? How will MarSupply look, Bard, when there's a shortage of Prime Vuervee?"

Bard shifted uncomfortably.

"How do you look, Dunt, with your MarSek force cowering in their boots? Fruke, you want to be remembered as the PR Councillor who lost the populous in a panic?"

Fruke's immense sihouette stared ahead.

Mr. Sir Blench's tiny, deepset eyes swept the rectangular meeting table. Blench wondered who was aligned with who. One never really knew.

Almost by definition, any Control Council featured a collection of Maurians who emerged atop a composte of diabolical cleverness and shrouded viciousness. Luck and ability were only the spicings.

So none were truly fooled or intimidated by Blench's threats. A crisis far smaller than this could blow the best from the SilverForm Office at 1W-1N. And then the puppets would dance, and when it was over the Control Council would have bright new faces. It was the way in which CityMauria evolved with the times through natural selection.

Blench wryly perused the group.

Sitting next to Fruke, Blench eyed Mr. Engineer—that is, Mr. *Sir* Engineer Rute, who was his usual silent self. These men of engineering science are so dull and quiet, thought Blench, so totally out the portal. It irked Blench, now as he thought back, that Rute's Sirship slipped through during his own vacation. Fruke said he mentioned it to him before he left. Blench didn't get it. Why would that help me, he thought? Keep an eye on those two.

Next to Rute sat Mr. Neff, the only commoner on the Council. His tallish, albino form supposedly represented the dwindling plight of the independent contractor and small gamer. Neff, impotent as an empty SonaGun, was really just a PR move to buffer opposition to Family Industries' runaway growth.

Next to Neff was Mr. Sir Bard, MarSupply, keeper of the food. A broad friendly face, a welcoming slap on the back to all, a trail of reeds in the back of anyone who took their eye off his smile . . . rumor had it.

And over here sat MarSek's Mr. Sir Dunt, Heroic leader of Mauria's Integritorial militia and security. His square-jawed, muscled body sat in it's usual stiff pose. A Hero. A Hero who used Black Materials in motivating a young scout to assassinate Dunt's predecessor . . . rumor said.

They all had their stories—well rumors.

And if this morning in the high Heroes' meeting room was fraught with dark uncertainty, it was a bright and warm early day for the Veem of Tedrin in the hills.

* * * * * * * * * * * * * *

Branches were opened to wombs, the food was already being gathered and prepared by early risers, and soon a meal of soaked cone Needletips, Pairflowers, bush apples and hot water from the warm spring river was savored against the morning chill.

There were many Vuervee who carried young, but none so ripe as Bobber, who waited the newday in her womb with Duerr.

More than a few on this finest yet of Spring days, awoke to the lovebite of mates.

Erduerr, a smallish bronze and green Vuerve—the Veem's foremost funplayer—was at his most energetic. He found his favorite friend, Grespuin. As small as Erduerr was, such was the tallness of Grespuin, whose reddish waisthair could scratch Enduerr's forehair.

Many sought this playful pair when their Circles spun hard. For Erduerr and Grespuin were light of mind, and their gleeful grins and voracious play could give one to mock of their own grimness.

To the chirping laughter of those about, Grespuin carted Erduerr about the Veem on shoulder.

Tedrin took Dillon's brothers, Venes and Hiola, on a climb to a peak known as Blue Ring.

Others searched the fleece-painted sky for path, and lazed on rocks or under trees, or splashed in the warm spring.

Sentia hummed tunes of minor, her clear voice kissing the gentle air. Javuerr and Brideae practiced vaulting, and Kieurr led a group to a new found climbing tree.

Much was well in the Veem of Tedrin on this day.

* * * * * * * * * * * * * *

Blue Ring was a peak of special love to the Vuervee. Every new Spring found a Circle of blue Mindo plants ringing the top of this tundra-coated ledge.

It was said that Blisfur—Mother to Tedrin; then later to Dillon, Venes and Hiola—Ended on this mountain, planting a Circle of seeds in the snow as her last beginning, her own Ended form nourishing life into the seeds on this otherwise barren bluff.

Dillon's two brothers, Venes and Hiola, stood near Blisfur's Circle on this rugged outbluff as Tedrin walked about the new buds in the ring of Mindo plants. Pinches of blue glimmered between the red baskets of budding leaves.

Earlier from far below, Tedrin had seen the faint, bluish glow of the blooming Mindo flowers and was beckoned.

What Sign was it that Dillon was nowhere to be found when Blisfur's blue seeds called to them?

Tedrin Mented to Dillon's brothers, Hiola and Venes.

The squat, blue and white Hiola, set his eyes to the sweeping snowpeaks which matched his white waisthair. His blue head and forehair stood in the breeze.

Now that snow melted even on the loftiest peaks, Hiola wanted Tedrin to take the Vuervee further from the Plains. Further from the Maurians.

Hiola wanted to be the perfect Vuerve, and even scolded other Vuervee for acting, in any small way, "un-Vuervenly." Hiola desired all thought and action to be as bright, simple and clear as the white peaks he now watched.

It was said of Hiola that he lived the Vuerven way with an unbending stiffness . . . almost the way a Maurian might have been a Vuerve.

And Tedrin knew why he was so, for he knew of Hiola's roots.

Tedrin's glance swung to Venes, the youngest brother. Slim Venes, a patch of rainbow colors against the gray Plains to the East, was as opposite from Hiola as the direction in which they gazed. Venes stared *toward* Mauria. Everlong, Venes had Mented to the Maurians, fascinated with their shiny tunics and devices, unhappy with the Vuervee's role of the hunted. Venes was of the Maurians like the child is of the fire—surely frightened, yet pulled toward it.

And Tedrin knew of this, too, and knew of its roots.

Yet one from this brood of Blisfur and the Maurian Kurk will guide his Veem soon, thought Tedrin.

Hiola stares far away to the wild snow peaks, Venes stares to the Maurian plains . . . and Dillon is not here at all!

And neither Mented to the ring of blue plants which their mother, Blisfur, left behind, to live.

"You do not Ment to Blisfur, Venes . . . .. Hiola?"

"I am not sure," said Venes, "she is here."

"You will not find her out there toward the Maurians where you look! She is here! But that you would Ment to her, you would both find her. This day. Here."

Hiola turned back to sweep the giant peaks.

Venes turned to Tedrin.

"You . . . know of my confusion," Venes pouted, stiff-lipped. "I wish not bad thoughts with you."

Tedrin leaned sharply to the taller, more fragile Venes. The red partial moon in the VeemVa's brown head hair seemed to flame brightly. As he spoke to Venes, his tone danced lightly atop a flower of pleading love, then cascaded to a deeper pool of dark and bubbling frustration.

"I am sad I wear upon you," Tedrin started. "It is of oversee. If you could love oversee as many do, your Circle would be. This ring of Mindo plants, Venes my love, is oversee, as is all. These flowers are a Circle created of many smaller Circles. Such is the world.

"All that is, can be seen in any part of what is. If you cannot find Blisfur in a walk through the forest, you cannot find her here, where her very flesh lives in these plants, Venes."

Tedrin beckoned to Hiola.

"If you cannot find your Circle in a small pebble, Hiola, you cannot find it in those huge snow peaks."

"You scold," Venes murmurred.

"I love. I teach. You are of Blisfur, like me. The Circle will choose you or Hiola or Dillon to begin my End as VeemVa, yet we see not together."

"Is it not of more growth," Venes tried, "for me to see my own Sign? I tire of all minds as one. . . I tire of running from the Maurians. We live in weakness! It is *they* who need *us*! Why do we crawl. . . "

"Venes! You speak *to* others, and not *for* them. We are, the Maurians are, the sky is, the trees are, . . .the Circle is."

"Yes," pleaded Venes, "but my Circle is unseen by yours."

"There is but a Circle! We do not find other Circles lying around like tree-cones! . . . If that you could see this, I could End with a smile!"

Tedrin stepped to Venes. He hugged him, then rubbed his forehair across Venes' cheek. Venes wept, but his eyes were angry.

Away from them, Hiola stared away and ahead. And the tallest peak spoke to him of a moment when the grand and wild peaks would become one with him, and he would fly through the air like the winged beings of a past time.

And then, this Sign told him, *all Vuervee would fly with him, proud, at last free.*

✳✳✳✳✳✳✳✳✳✳✳✳✳✳

The Control Council emergency meeting had droned on until 500Time middle day.

"But reason," said Mr. Sir Bard of MarSupply, "speak to a Vuervee!? Communicate with a future *meal?*"

Blench's SilverForm Wig was unyielding.

"It *does* appear that as distasteful as it may be, a meeting may be the only Array. Fruke?"

Mr. Sir Fruke's gargantuan face nodded and shook.

"Whatso, Heroes!" Fruke boomed. "*I* must admit to a certain delightful anticipation, the sheer idea of it. Everso, if we can manipulate high Heroes like Maurians with PR, . . . well *imagine* what my MarPrex could do with a lowly animal's mind!"

They all nodded and clicked their metal boot-heels on the alloy floor. Soon the echoes of the pounding clicks faded down.

Blench was annoyed to notice Mr. Neff, who had dropped into a sleep at the end of the meeting table. Commoner dirt, anyso.

One more annoyance: why did that engineer Rute of EnvirCo keep so silent through all this? And why did the large black eyes of Rute and Fruke sometimes latch together for a shadowy nod? Whatso? Or was he just tired, bleary? Who knew?

Blench's feet were starting to chafe raw from sweat against his boots' inner alloy. The cursed boot vents must be plugged again.

"Heroes," Blench intoned, "we are set on our path to high Integritorial Array. We will go to the Vuerven animals and we will meet with them, or do with them whatever we must, to reclaim . . . the Integrity which they have so unHeroicly stolen through this most

. . . lowly deed."

Now Blench stood and slammed his hand on the table.

"Or the SilverForm Wig falls from my head!"

There were moments of such emotion when all Heroes dropped their twisting allegiances, their schemes, their personal ambitions.

This was one of them. All the Heroes of the Council, even the newly awakened Mr. Neff, stood and clicked their boots and slammed their fists.

And they were united as one in their resolve. And they all sensed great Heroism in their leader, Mr. Sir Councillor Blench, and a lump of proud Maurian Integrity swelled in their throats.

CHAPTER NINE
'A Spring Snow'

Dillon blinked his cached eyes. His form had bowed over a low branch during the night. The new day was sunny, but large clouds encroached, and this rapid white coating could only mean a Spring squall. The air was cooling very fast.

Dillon wondered at the dark beauty of the rolling formations; the tingling cool dampness that saturated body and bone. He shivered.

The formations of storm clouds awakened his imagination and he saw shapes: there was a young face twisting above him; and a river over there. The visions contracted as the smokey-white strata flowed by.

A drop of wet snow spattered his nose, blurring his vision. He glanced up to the rising sun, prismed by the water in his eye: and the sun's light broke into the spread of the rainbow, the full range of colors fanned out in his misted eye.

Dillon knew this was a Sign. For in this fan of colors between red and purple, there was a white arc where the blue should be. Up away from the rainbow this color blue hung above, detached from its home. A flash of green beckoned from a distance, also aloof from the rainbow.

This blue color split further from the rest, moving upwards and towards the flash of green. Dillon's eye cleared, and he looked at his own waisthair and knew it was his blue, and that he must seek a Sign away from his Veem, his friends.

But he knew he would End or begin on this next Sign . . . and could see and speak to no one until it came.

He walked up a hill, away from the Vuervee, away from the Maurians. His blue form raised over a meadow, whose Spring flowers showed the colors of the rainbow.

Then the clouds claimed the Sun.

* * * * * * * * * * * * *

Of all in the Veem of Tedrin, there was a Vuerve whose Circle of survival was so strong that he was known to seek the Maurian hunters, so that he may lead a hunted Vuerven friend to safety.

He was Duerr. His fore, head and waisthair were rusty red. He had a wealth of slash marks on his already craggy and wise face, these from fleeing through whipping branches and Maurian darts, over many changes. He was reed-thin, and had a form meant for marks and scars. They complimented the bony features, the tendons.

His most loved effort had lost him an arm, in the saving of a large group of young during Maurian FieldDay last. On that day, he took a dart in his arm. Knowing of the poison, he managed to sever his wounded limb with a Maurian reed he always carried.

He abandoned this part of him, in a thick Torna plant, and led the young to a cave. The hunters took the rest of the day to surround Duerr's arm, while he and the young had escaped.

But this day, his boney, scar-veined face smiled warmly upon Bobber, and his thoughts were away from hunters and survival.

Bobber was of warm, soft brown colorhair; and fair, white skin which took little browning from the Sun. And now, middle swelled with brood, her nut-brown eyes stared, unwavering to Duerr.

He fed strength into her eyes, from his eyes. He squeezed hope into her soul with his hand.

Bobber felt the first life-filled waterbag slip from between her arced legs. Her face was peaceful, taut. Tears dribbled down her rounded chin to her sweat-soaked neck. She wept softly into Duerr's eyes. There was some pain, and much happiness.

Duerr's face became hard set. His scars turned bright red from within as he strained against Bobber's arms, and helped her to push.

And then another young dropped to the soft bed of fresh, Spring leaves; and then another, and then another, and finally another.

In Bobber's face, he could see her love for him, for the lake of his strength. And this fanned the flames of his purpose, his hope, his love.

He forced the aftercords and foodbags down Bobber's frightened throat. She would need these for strength. Duerr carefully slit the waterbag from about the young and managed to do all this, and more, with his single arm. The liquid gushed from each opened bag into a bowl made of Sun-baked earth. This and all birth water was saved for healing sickness and wounds.

A small amount would be pushed through a hole into some hollow nuts, then sealed in the Sun. As the nut dried and shrunk, the hole sealed, and each young would wear this Birthgem all through life. Sometimes, other matter was put into the Birthgem with the water, like seeds or a patch of forehair.

After Duerr had given Bobber her young to lick clean and hold, the strain upon Bobber's gritted mouth melted away, and a peaceful calm of loving gratefulness settled in the womb.

They stared at the tiny, bald, wriggling young, who soon were still in sleep.

"Who," gasped Bobber, "do they look like?"

"Happy for them," grinned the craggy Duerr, "you."

Above them the womb covered with Spring snow. Inside, exhausted and happy, Bobber and Duerr fell asleep, the morning to show the Veem their proud Brood.

But Tedrin had watched through the portal, and was already spreading the happy word.

The snow swirled harder, as the deepening cold drew steam from the warm spring nearby. Each tree and plant shrugged under a cloak of wet, spring snow, a last reminder of the dying Winter.

* * * * * * * * * * * * * *

To be sure, reproduction in CityMauria had little resemblance to that of the Vuervee. In fact, in the time it took Bobber to deliver four young— Maurian couples and collectors had bought and sold, and bought again, probably 80,000 BookCredits worth of Maurian Extracts in the LifeCo Hall of Futures.

Right now, it was 700Time in Mauria, and The Hall of Futures was at its peak of activity.

Actual vials of Extracts—as well as future strains described in LifeCo data sheets—were being shouted and screamed for in the cavernous alloy hall.

The large SonaBoard, which yielded instantaneous changes, quotes and prices, glittered and blinked with rapid-fire updates.

One Mr. who was intent on the large board was Mr. Granes. Having long since recovered from his bout at the small gaming Parlor of Bordt, Granes scribbled primary bids on an x-3 series of Extract, said to be in the blood line of 76 Mr. Sirs.

There was also a broad sampling of Misters who, with their Ladies, were thoughtfully picking the particular brands of Extract to compliment the woman's features and background.

Many such couples chose to visit a councillor in one of the many brightly colored booths, there to have an expert help form an Integritorial choice.

Many CommonerMales watched from a sectioned-off area, learning the peculiar dialect and nomenclature of LifeCo's marketing— hoping one day they would achieve Mr.Ship and get a Lady of their own for whom to bid Extract.

Atop the hall sat LifeCo's Councillor, Mr. Sir Burn, keeping an unswerving eye on his own miniature SonaBoard. Sales must be kept within birth futures, and a long list of other restrictions.

Many UniMeters from LifeCo, at Burn's private home, his own Lady was shouting much like the shoppers below him, but not to bid on Extract.

* * * * * * * * * * * * * *

Lady Burn hovered over the smallish CommonerFemale like a dark cloud, bobbing and darting her head with each verbal thrust at the wispy girl. Lady Burn was a touch overweight, even for a Maurian Lady—she had been remiss in visiting the health rooms lately—and this superfluous matter shook with the more venomous words.

"Grell! Curse you!" She was really boiling. "I waited for you at the InterFare since 400Time. And it was properly cold out there! If you forgot to show up, you could have had the politeness to create a plausible excuse so I wouldn't know you had not given me a thought! What is so hard about saying 'I was suddenly taken ill, Lady,' or any number of polite fabrications you owe a Lady! You're lucky Mr. Sir wasn't here!"

Young Trebel shook beneath this viperous attack. How Trebel despised Ladies—they didn't even bother with CounterFlow when it came to commoners. Moreso, they usually exploded what they held back in higher company, thus Trebel was obviously getting a bonus.

Out of one WorkHouse, into another, thought Trebel.

Her thin, smallish frame cowered beneath Lady Burn's fury, and shriveled under the heftier authority and Maurian stature.

"What kind of a name is Trebel, anyso?! That can't be your real name!"

"It was Treb, my friends at the . . . "

"Treb is a perfectly acceptable name, it even does <u>you</u> justice. Trebel? That is as low as that stupid ForeBar you're wearing! It's too small to even see the design. What is it, a child's ForeBar?!"

Trebel's face reddened, highlighting patches of freckles. "Please, Lady, my forehead isn't yet large enough for . . . "

"If you're not old enough to dress properly," Lady Burn's rancor started to drain, "you shouldn't be working yet."

"But you see, Lady . . . "

"I see too much as it is, young Trebel! You've no further use here."

"But Lady, they'll send me back to the WorkHouse," she was trying to hide a large lobe of tear running down her nose. "Please give me another chance. I'll do. . . "

"You'll do nothing. Get out. Report back to your overseer, and if you don't make mention of how understanding I've been I'll tell him you cried, too. Then you'll never get out! How dare you cry in front of me!"

Young Trebel rushed all her CounterFlow together at once, wiping the petty emotion from her face. Integrity, she thought. Integrity was the basis of life. Her resolve lasted through the portal, down the FareWay, till just before the drop. Then she looked around and was overcome.

She ducked under the platform to a shiny supply dock, and bawled her head off. She thought of a MarSekMan seeing her like this, and then imagined another stint in the WorkHouse. It made her sob harder.

She felt the icy chill of a cold front blow down the FareWay. And then she stopped crying, and thought:

What if I don't go back!

The very uniqueness of the thought sent tremors through her mind. What if she just, well, ran away?! Forgot it all! Forgot about CounterFlow. Forgot about reporting in. Forgot about hiding that stupid green streak in her hair with BlackForm dye. Forgot about overeating to pad her thin form. Just forgot!

* * * * * * * * * * * * *

Mr. Sir Burn pulled 12Book, handed it to the commoner attendant, and slid into his SonaRail. His body ached from the long session at the Hall of Futures.

Whatso, he thought, another day. And, from the look of those mean, gray clouds blowing in, a good one to spend inside. This late snow would never survive the furnaced atmosphere covering Mauria, but the cold would. The wind. Already his metal tunic was transmitting the cold into his skin.

What happened to Spring?

Burn had been Councillor of LifeCo for four years. Impeccable manners, uncanny skill at compromise and CounterFlow had Integritorily fused to evolve his career above all others in his field. His scientific training had *helped*, but B-1 scientists were common as FareBeams. *He* was a Hero. To the people. To himself.

He switched to FareWay 76N, and the SonoRail hooked onto the beam.

Once, he remembered, he had gone to the EdgeHills and recorded a view of all Mauria with his corder. The Sun then had been low, and had reliefed all the shiny FareBeams. The picture showed a cross-work of thousands of FareBeams in perfect parallel and right angles, as indeed Mauria was. Perfect, thought Burn. A wonderful city.

The view had won a place on the wall of Blench's eating room, and certainly hadn't hurt during his final elevation to Councillor of LifeCo. It was the little extras that culled one from the herd, nodded Burn.

His SonoRail jolted harshly at InterFare 25W-67N. A MarSek vehicle slid through, the two men inside engaged in a game of Terrain. Curse those dithers! For what they are paid . . . But even at this irritation, it was difficult to see anything but acceptance—friendly at that—in his wide, easy face.

Burn pressed his message Box. A few complaints. Parents always screamed when their genetic plans didn't quite actualize. Most popular game in the city, Burn lamented, blaming offspring failings on LifeCo. They knew their risk, they signed away recourse when they bid on the Extract! Yet still they tried. Everso.

He sympathized with them, naturally. After all, full education on predictability—or unpredictability—of maturing children would be disastrous to sales. Better they blamed themselves.

Burn considered himself a nice man. He had always done anything that was *feasible* to make Maurian life more enjoyable. His scientific make-up loathed the blackreeding and scheming texture of the other high Heroes. He did only what he *had* to, in defense.

And, he chuckled, few have felt the teeth of his "defense" and lived to tell another.

As he programmed a right turn onto FareWay 25W, his wandering eye rested on a young CommonerGirl, whose age troubled him. She had the stature of an adult, yet her slim features suggested a mere child. Rare, that one, he thought. Very skinny. Ah, to be unencumbered by all this weight! To live the long years of a Vuerve, those poor animals!

Burns SonoRail, with its bright "LifeCo" insignia, whirred around the corner, into the blowing dusk.

* * * * * * * * * * * * * *

Trebel started when the expensive LifeCo SonoRail cruised by. The well-dressed Mr. Sir within seemed to stare at her, but he continued around the corner, out of sight.

Her features radiated tension. She had little business walking to higher numbered Fares down 25W, and the MarSek SonoRails whisking by appeared to study her longer.

A steady drive of chilly air blew at her, driving the steam from the SonaVents quickly up. The West wall of Mauria ribboned from afar. Her service tunic was a weak match for the icy gusts, which peeled Mauria's atmosphere cloud.

When she reached InterFare 25N-136W, she felt even more exposed.

This far West, near MarSek outposts, commoners were unique. So was anyone walking.

At 25N-144W she watched a MarSek slave vehicle screech to a stop, the metal smell of alloy brakes on alloy FareBeam drifted a pungent wake to her numbing, freckled nose.

A security officer unloaded. The MarSekMan was too hurried to notice her as he ran through the icy wind into a building with shiny gray supports offsetting the buffered metal of the main structure.

Her shivering body stiffened as her eyes riveted on the gleaming lines of the dart-shaped SonaRail. Everything about it spoke of movement, speed, freedom. Freedom even beyond FareBeams. It spoke of action!

And she sensed that *action* was her course. Young Trebel was swept by visions of hunting Heroes from book adventures, titillated by the energy of escape, disgusted at the possibility of the WorkHouse. She began shaking and quivering again, and suddenly dashed into the FareWay.

Not fully understanding, she leapt to the outer shell of the empty MarSek SonoRail. The storm-cooled alloy stung her hands.

She concentrated. Oddly, her mind was icy clear as she processed options. Either the MarSekMan would rejoin the slave SonoRail, or he wouldn't. If he didn't, where would the vehicle head? Back to mid-Mauria, or even further West?

Must decide, what is my answer? My answer is, . . . best use of slave SonoRails is unity of motion. A string of stops in one direction . . . West!

She jumped into the vehicle and pushed at the multi-colored buttons which banked across the control panel.

A jolt answered her. The vehicle slid ahead and picked up speed as it headed West, the mountains coming into view over the West wall; and Trebel's young mind wondered at this deed. She didn't know herself, and fear washed through her soul, and she knew it was too late to go back, anyso.

Yet, she was pulsating with a rush of clear, strong purpose . . . feeling in control of something for the first time in her life.

* * * * * * * * * * * * * *

Most Maurians weathered the initial cold wedge of the Spring storm inside. A trip on the SlideWalks could well be delayed until Mr. Sir Rute of EnvirCo deemed it time to unleash the big furnace.

Not so the fifty-two Students of Mr. Professor Gribb's Level B-2 class, who finally disrobed Winter tunics, and cursed their walk from the drop. When icy winds blew into metallic Mauria, the buildings and FareWays acted like MarSupply's freezer coils, absorbing the cold degree for degree.

"Never happier to be in classes," clucked one student.

Far across town, ParlorMan Bordt hoisted a "closed" sign over the portal to his gaming room. One could always count on a Spring snow to dull the edge of trade.

And across town again, Mr. Sir Engineer Rute eagerly awaited the MarPrex press group, for Mauria's large SonaFurnace was being primed. It always gave him a thrill to hear of impending weather, because he would get all-Maurian coverage. Bad weather also drove most Maurians to their homes—near their home screens!

A twisted assembly of MarPrex Corders, wires, lights and workers rustled in readiness for the close shot of Rute's finger depressing the "Heroic Switch," which would release volumes of stored heat from the SonaFurnace.

The same script would be enacted. The same soothing, excitable statement: "We have hopes of coming within .002 of projected output," Rute would say.

Rute licked his lips. An oversized panel light glowed "ready." The MarPrex press Corders focused on his massive, inverted forehead, which extended enough to cast a shadow over his eyes and nose. He had chosen an extra large, triangular ForeBar to emphasize his features.

Yes, Rute was riding a building wave of PR and achievement to Heroism. In the last period, Mauria had suffered the lowest number of Oxygen poisoning deaths ever! Well, if you believed the press releases.

Rute wore Integrity well. His stoic, deep-clefted face gracefully welcomed Heroics and praise as if they were long-expected guests.

Now, with this Westerly storm drifting in, the CO2 furnaces would convert to heat exhaustion—the normal *waste* of the burners becoming the *product*! Uncountable Solarenes of heat rushing through all nerve ducts in Mauria, blanketing the immediate atmosphere with enough heat to turn the snow into steam which harmlessly drifted out to the plains.

Savings from ten years ago: 2,000,000Book per year! He remembered the way it used to be: All night SonoPlows endlessly tapping energy as they opened Fares. The wasted Solarenes used to pump CO2 through the driving rains or snow. The absence of reserve atmosphere, and the overBook paid to crews.

Rute retained the longest tenure of anyone on the Control Council, save for Blench. Unless the world caved in, he would be next for the SilverForm Wig—Head of the Control Council and of all Mauria.

And prepared he was. Prepared to meet and defeat the natural contempt Maurians would have for the first leader from the Engineering world. Prepared for the pressure, the loneliness of the highest Hero.

The SilverForm Wig.

Now, Rute sulked, if he could only deal with that Grellsnip Granes! Imagine, being black-reeded by a common fiftieth some-odd Mr. of LifeCo.

A lowly fool with Black Materials over him. Curse!

And for what? For nothing of *his* doing! Mauria only gave to commoners one arena for upward mobility—engineering. And then to hold his background against him!

Evenso, Rute had piece by piece erased his history, changed it; constantly living in Grell-eating poverty so his BookCredits could buy a new past. Amidst the expensive Black Materials, the scheming, he had still managed to study, to innovate technology!

He had huffed and scratched, and he had raised his roots to within a small hair of total Integrity.

And that was Granes, that hair. For Granes had been in class with Rute as a child. Rute still remembered the very day he had failed his third and final Integrity screening. He relived the reed of sinking terror, for he had then thought that Mr.Ship was forever out of his reach.

He had walked to the drop with a young Granes and spoke of it—had cried at knowing he was now a commoner, and thought he would be everso. His one mark. His one indiscretion, and how it had flourished and grown like a black tree in the dark.

More than ten YearMaurias later, Rute and Granes met again as LifeCo trainees seeking Mr. Ship. Rute had used that century to fight off the shackles and climb out, and up.

Granes had used it to fail, fail and fail again. So that as their paths had crossed from opposite directions—up and down— Granes had used the advancing Rute's past to halt his own deadfall. Help me out, Granes had demanded, or I'll show your past.

And still, Rute thought, I rose, even with Granes as drag weight! He had had to use his own influence to insure Granes' advancement and security in LifeCo.

Bad enough to roll in dirt . . . but to taste it, too!

And really, he asked himself—how long would it be before Granes tired of the comfortable life of an unspectacular mid-Mr.? How long before Rute would get the next call on his CompBox: " . . . I'm sure many Heroes would find your school records rather interesting, *Mr. Sir* Rute. *CommonerMale* Rute . . . ”

A sure bid for trouble, he shook his head.

It just wasn't fair.

A voice broke Rute's ponderings.

“Excuse me,” chimed an energetic young MarPrex newsman, “The Corders are ready, Mr. Engin . . . Mr. Sir Engineer Rute. Figure on pushing the big switch 40Time from now, sir.”

* * * * * * * * * * * * * * *

Day dreaming was another of Trebel's problems. This time she had become enraptured with a vision of herself—living the life of a hunter Hero from a book adventure, living in caves, hunting Vuervee with but a sharpened pole, sleeping under the stars. She would be a legend.

In this dollydream, the unMaurian streak of green in her hair became a proud Hero's mark, flaming in the wild wind! Her thin form, always embarrassing, now gave her speed to outrun even a Vuerve!

And she returned to Mauria a Hero. The Maurians celebrated their first-ever Lady Hero with a Parade of endless Integrity. Trebel . . . the legend!

Her legend was interrupted by the jolt of the slave MarSek SonoRail stopping before one of the MarSek huts she had seen in pictures, which outpost Mauria. Security Heroes of high rank, with all their probe equipment, lived here, she knew. Time for little miss legend to hop off her historical dream.

“Perhaps an explanation is in order, young one!” boomed a large, male voice.

Trebel's reflex reaction was to scream and leap through the open roof of the SonaRail, trying to escape—but her service tunic caught on a metal lip, and she fell down the rear of the vehicle, bumping onto the FareBeam. The metal railing bruised her tailbone, and she cried out in pain.

"Let's look here," the man said as he pressed his hand into the small of her back. "No problem. It will hurt for a while, though. Whatso! Plenty of good medical care in the WorkHouse!"

The bright letters of MarSek glimmered from his medal-crusted tunic. He had a clean, alloy-like face honed of confidence. His friendly, saturating authority made Trebel feel foolish, impotent.

What's your name?" he grinned.

"Tober," she lied.

"I'm Gurnt, Level2 MarSek. You'll sleep here tonight in my quarters and then I'll escort you personally to the WorkHouse tomorrow. Should have some good snow tomorrow, eh? Follow me, please."

Gurnt turned towards his quarters, and as Trebel followed she heard the regimented clip-clop of his jewel alloy heels echoing against the West wall, just a stone's toss away.

And just on the other side, so close, the freedom beckoned.

"The SonoRail is for me to use tomorrow, Tober, and now I'll have a partner, eh?"

His laugh gurgled through an unusually curved neck. "See these bowls, Tober?"

He turned to show her a pile of decorated bowls. They were cupped from dried earth, obviously of Vuerven making.

"We find these in abandoned Vuerve camps. I collect them. They have something to do with births."

She gazed up to his eyes, looming half a body over hers. He wore no ForeBar, and she thought he was rather handsome.

He crossed to open the door.

When he turned back to allow her to pass ahead, an authentic, decorated Vuerven bowl slammed into his temple.

He was dead before he hit the ground, and young Trebel looked upon his body, her own shaking in the cold night air.

The rest was a blurred dream for Trebel.

Time ebbed and shrunk. Everywhile or so she caught a view of her arms as she tugged MarSekMan Gurnt into his outpost hut, an immense chore for her worn body.

But she felt no strain. Her flickering eyes absorbed dreamy threads of the interior surroundings—a WeatherSensor here, a map of the EdgeHills there, a communications Corder there.

After she had managed to pull Gurnt's corpse part way across the quarters, Trebel looked at him. He did not bleed. His color was pale. A small network of bluish veins was all that labeled the point of impact.

An odd grin formed as she realized she was in complete wide-eyed mellow, peaceful shock.

Suddenly there was a giant shoooooosh! from somewhere outside. She wondered why she didn't jump from the sudden noise.

Far across Mauria, Rute had pushed the big switch, and the monster furnace was exploding heat through all the SonaVents in the city—cooking the atmosphere to ward off the snow storm moving at Mauria.

But Trebel's mind was in her dollydream. Ahah, she thought, the wind had blown the West wall down! Ho-ho, another obstacle gone between her and freedom. The great and Heroic Lady Trebel!

Trebel rested her head on the floor, her muscles spent. She must leave instantly . . . yes, instantly.

The floor softened and soon felt like the soft bed of a Lady. She was so tired. So scared . . . she had killed a MarSekMan. Her eyelids were feeling quite heavy, and she was, after all, exhausted from this adventure.

As she imagined dashing outside and away to freedom, young Trebel passed into deep sleep; her book-adventure smile not a breath away from Gurnt's ever surprised, bluing lips.

* * * * * * * * * * * * * * *

Early Sun danced playfully over the Veem of Tedrin and filtered bars of radiance shafted into the slits of Bobber and Duerr's hut. The storm clouds had slid past the mountains in the night and could be seen billowing above the Plains to the East.

Duerr and Bobber shifted awake. They were in a tangled web with the newborn young, who still slept. It was a sticky, messy, happy pile of life. Earlier, Tedrin and Hiola had quietly straightened inside the hut, removed the decorated earthen bowls which held the birth water, and left a feast of early meal by the mound of sleeping forms.

Many of the Veem were buzzing with play this bright morning. Last night's storm had left a thin carpet of glimmering white, even upon new buds. There was much romping in the already melting Winter's visit to Spring.

When Duerr and Bobber finally emerged from the womb portal, each holding a pair of young to show, the entire Veem awaited them. They formed a Circle around Duerr and Bobber, and Dausent's melody tube sent a fragile tune through the sky.

Each friend who made this Circle wore a round wreath upon their hand, made of needles and tied in small Circles.

Ganura and Seudra, perched high atop the tallest trees, released a sea of the Senta plant's spinning seeds. As these flying seeds were carried by approving breeze, the sky bubbled and lit from this golden cloud.

Many of the Veem of Tedrin, feeling their Circles spin gloriously above their own forms, sang to the world. It was a day of love in the mountains, . . . and the storm had moved on, to Mauria.

* * * * * * * * * * * * * * *

"BLEEEEEE-UP! . . . . BLEEEEEEEEEEEEPAH!" The noxious noise jarred Trebels' peaceful swoon. She fought to calm her ears, and pulled an imaginary cover overhead.

"BLEEEEEEE-UP! . . . . .BLEEEEEEEEEEEEPAH!"

Grell! she fumed, but she was too dizzy to stand at first.

The room swayed. This was not the usual morning reticence. Even when she staggered to the WallCorder to stifle the raking beep, she couldn't fan alertness into her veins. Something was wrong.

She glanced over the rather complicated comp machine and hesitated at different toggle switches. One said "Akng." Acknowledge? She flipped the switch and the bleeping stopped.

A female voice, obviously recorded, said, "Thank you for promptly acknowledging, Hero Gurnt. Make today's itinerary now. Thank you."

Curse! Now they'll know for sure.

"If there is something wrong, Hero Gurnt, explain now," said the voice, "or we will notify MarSek Control. Please answer."

She saw a mirror and was startled to see her frazzled features looking back, a complete stranger.

"For your protection," the voice droned on, "we have notified MarSek, and . . . "

Next to the reflection, though, was Gurnt's CO_2 cord. Fool! she scolded. You would have wandered merrily over the wall, and died from the Oxygen. That explained the unrelenting dizziness, the fogginess. Indeed, the strong winds had probably brought waves of poisonous Oxygen into this perimeter area.

She stuffed the cord in her nose, snapped the CO_2 cartridge on her belt, and sat on an alloy stool. Slowly, her brain cleared, her limbs felt stronger.

With clarity, the panic returned.

Trebel leapt out the front portal, then stopped, turning back. Think, think . . .

She went back inside and looked quickly around. She ran to the shelf and removed a coil and hook; dashed to the closet and pulled a pair of soft metal gloves from a cubbyhole, putting them on.

Now, back outside.

She turned toward the wall and began to run. Glimpsing the mountains in the distance, she noticed they were white with snow never to fall on Mauria. A few flakes made it near the ground, but steaming SonaVents dissipated them.

She tried to remember, what was it? Oh, yes, "Hero Dren." In that adventure he refilled C02 from plants. Or was it fires? Silly to think now; she'd remember soon enough, or she wouldn't.

Trebel threw her coil over the West wall, the hook clanging on the metal lip. Concentration replaced nervousness, excitement replaced fear. As she scurried up the wall, a whooosh! from the nearest EnvirCo SonaVent started her momentarily.

Ho-hi, the luck, she realized. MarSekMen would not venture from the affected climate into the snow. Most Maurians would panic without a FareBeam, anyso! Ha!

From the top of the alloy-shingled wall, she had to jump twice her height to the ground. When she landed, the first snowflakes she had felt in years splashed the bridge of her nose. She laughed with drunken joy, and sheer childish elation soaked her soul.

The further she dashed from the dark outline of Mauria, the more vibrant she felt. The wind! The space! Vignettes of book adventures flashed across her eyes.

She turned to take last look at the hated life of Mauria, her lips grimacing in proud disdain. She never fit. As if to punctuate this thought a long lock of her hair fell before her eyes, the sleet washing the black dye, exposing green. These strands of colored hair flaired in blatant contrast to the grayish squalor of steam--beshrouded Mauria.

But what is that small light above the wall?

MarSekMen! Well, you fools, it's too late now. *I'm* not afraid of the snow! A cocky, satisfied grin crumpled her face.

Trebel turned to the onrushing snow, legs pumping fast. As she did so, there was a pinch on her arm. When had she felt this before? The answer registered, and shook her very bones: A sleep dart!

"You rotting Grell!" she screamed.

But there was a chance. They had fired before she turned, and she would not receive the full dose from her arm-wound. Must run as far as I can before . . . .

She ran and ran and ran, feet hurtling rocks and plants. Each stride was a length of freedom.

Could she get far enough?

Soon she was running in slow-motion, the snowflakes were dreamy bits of tunic lace sent to comfort her wound.

Her legs flew light and soft, softer . . . lighter . . .

She was surprised to see the snowy ground rising to her face, and barely moved her arm in time to break the fall.

Her mouth dropped open, stupidly, the drug was winning. She cursed the Maurians. She started to wiggle back up, when her legs claimed her attention. She giggled as her leg twitched about, swathing sprays of snow. It was all so funny, now.

Ho-de-hi, ho-de-hi,
I'm young Trebel, if you want to know . . .

By the time a crust of snow piled upon Trebel's brow, she was roasting in the warmth of book adventure dreams.

A quiet wind, spent from storming, dusted flakes about the Plains.

Just in a fold of the first EdgeHill, the outline of a sleeping young girl was shaped in the snowdust.

And back in CityMauria, Heroes high and low, were cozy in their abodes, as the storm engulfed the city.

CHAPTER TEN
'Searchings'

Dillon, in a forest beneath Blue Ring, leaned against a tree. He had climbed and wandered all the day, for this dwarfed woods was beshrouded in steamy clouds. The mist gently washed through the lonely stands of timber, swirls of water beads wound between branches. Loneliness and beauty combined for bittersweet reflection, and his thoughts battered his confused mind from all places at once.

Would that a Sign would come! I am learning what no Vuerve can learn, to hate myself. I have done what no Vuerve can do. To kill another is to kill yourself.

Dear, dear Circle, if I am here . . . then I am you! And I have killed. And you will speak to me now. Now! You will tell me why this is! It is I who is wrong, not the Circle.

Yet all is of the Circle, even me! Is there no Circle? Is there no me?!

Dillon plunged to the ground carpet and rubbed his face through the snow to the dirt. The smell, the grit—the Spring of his tears— soothed his spirit. He clutched at the ground, as to find the core of all life beneath.

I shall seek your Sign, he vowed. I will search till I am found. The storm in his soul passed, for now.

He climbed more, and now was at Blue Ring. He moved the snow from the patch of blue flowers which Blisfur had planted so long ago. Blisfur, he pleaded, what strange branch of life have you given me? Or did I take it as I took the life of another?

I must have my Sign! If this Sign tells of my Ending, he thought, then I will bless it if it makes me whole . . . and know of all things.

But no Sign was coming this day for the tormented Dillon, on these waves of cloud, above a still carpet of quiet snow.

His heart quieted, once more.

Dillon walked back down towards the valleys, there to continue his search to be found by the Circle.

To the beginning.

To the truth.

＊＊＊＊＊＊＊＊＊＊＊＊＊＊

Young Trebel giggled. She was positioned on a grassy knoll in an EdgeHill West of Mauria. She must have stumbled just far enough from the wall for them to think they missed her, that she had made it away clean. It was good fortune, indeed, that she had crumpled in a fold of ground, out of sight.

She was still woozy from the sleep dart, but was alert enough to take stock:

She had a good supply of CO_2, her tube was in perfect condition. Food would be no problem—not here in Vuerve-country!

She must remember how to make a fire, "Hero-Dren" style. Fire! That was it. All she had to do was set her cartridge near the fire, and it would fill it's little self with CO_2. And upon flushing through her tube, it would be refined to wholesome air!

She chuckled when she thought of Mauria. Half of the Maurians would have an attack if they knew someone left by *choice*.

The WorkHouse. All that slush about "remolding" oneself for the Heroic Maurian world. Anyone, they said, could become a Hero. Even a WorkHouse commoner.

The WorkGuards, with their sing-song measure sticks for

life—then the same Heroes throwing her to the floor, Mating their very words!

Her freckled, upturned nose crinkled at these memories. Her mischievous mouth snarled disgust. Her greenish-black eyes, though, danced giddily; because now—alone—she was more content than ever. She laughed and marched off to the West!

To book adventure!

* * * * * * * * * * * * * * *

At 1N-1W, behind the Silver door, in the Silver decorated office of the SilverForm Wig, Mr. Sir Blench felt his stomach jump as the first meeting plans poured to his desk. He had gamed all Book on this Vuerven meeting.

He popped another sour candy into his pursing mouth.

Ironically, uniqueness would have be his ally, compromise his forgotten warrior. His Heroic Councillorship was on the line. But whatso? He had slim choice. Events had transpired, and a boiling vacuum had emerged.

This was more than ample breeding ground for treachery, for plotted upheaval. This was *not* the moment for turning to "faithful" advisors. A reed in the back might ensue, or *is* ensuing!

There were other reasons for going CounterFlow. Unrest was the enemy. Maurian unrest. It is like none other. It could come from long months of boring news, or a suggestion of challenge to Maurian Integrity, or a stagnant economy, or a lack of spectacular scientific discovery, or it could even burst from nothing whatsoever. A civilization of fighters, hunters, and discoverers rested not. Everso . . .

In this instance it came from some of everything. A complicated whorl of particles that spelled change. And change spelled disaster for high Heroes.

First, there was that uncoverable Vuerven murder of an

Integritorial Maurian hunter. Gossip had created rumors worse than the real event.

Killer Vuervee stalking the hills, indeed.

Then, that stupid affair at the wall. A spit of a CommonerGirl had murdered a high ranked MarSekMan, escaped from Mauria, and she wasn't even armed! Whatso?!

Again, the Integrity of all Mauria challenged; and again, Fruke *conveniently* unable to muffle the event in PR. So. Hmmmnn . . . Fruke and . . . who else?

And the economy, too. A minor dip. Of course hunting was down, with those Grell-bound rumors of "killer Vuervee" out there. Naturally, MarSupply would edge off a little! And of course the number of Prime Vuerven dinners would decrease somewhat.

All these elements added up to one truth: CityMauria was starting to stale like a stagnant, explosive puddle . . . with a fire under it.

And that TeleCording of some stupid Vuerven ceremony North-West of Mauria. Why did those press men report it as a kind of war pomp. Impossible! But again, Fruke was remiss in snuffing these eroding reports. Back reeder.

Mr. Sir Blench could not think of when his tenacious power bloc had wobbled so. And there was no one to help but himself. A rare state of affairs for this Councillor of CityMauria!

Even petty Mating was up this year. The problem with attaining the high Heroship was you were blamed by the public for crimes you couldn't *possibly* have anything to do with!

Animals.

* * * * * * * * * * * * * *

It was 91Time in the morning. A small antique CompBox glowed upon a file-heaped counter. Records of news stories adorned the tinny frame of a reflector. It was the room of an old scientist. An old scientist who didn't turn in last year's CompBox for a metal-smelling new one—whose light fixtures bore scratches, stains, even dust. In fact, this room contained the one element most of Mauria considered disgusting, . . . the past.

Mr. Scientist Crilp had been cleaning out old EnvirCo files. His sixty-six years had etched deep rivers of study in his ancient face. As one who had exceeded the average Maurian lifespan, he had lately been rustled by a desperate twinge for a last Heroic discovery. Not that he hadn't made contributions, understand. And how close he had come to Heroics.

His jowls cast great shadows on his transparency desk. His shiny note records reflected his bulging, drooping face. His eyes, a middle black, conveyed kindness, or a certain softness.

He came across the capsule labelled, "*LifeCo Contract: Body Hybrid Modification. +P+U+R+P+O+S+E+ to modify existing Maurian Body Characteristics For the Purpose of Streamlining Form Without Economic Loss to MarSupply.*"

As he unrolled the case history, he reflected upon this turning point in his career. At the age of seventeen, he had already been medalled for significant contribution. He was to become a Hero any time.

While some thought it premature, he had been one of twenty-six assigned to the vital task of modifying Maurian body structure for LifeCo. To raise the Maurian physical form to a new level!

The others had hired investigators. It was a mad rush to locate the Maurian whose Extract could be the prototype. The catalyst-mutation which might evolve over 250 years!

Abandoning policy, Mr. Scientist Crilp had crammed day and night, and day and night for months. His competition engaged in elaborate MarPrex releases of suspected breakthoughs, human interest releases about childhoods.

And then his heroic brainstorm! Why Grell around? For years the Maurians had been envious of Vuerven form. Why not combine? Yes, combine!!

Sleepless weeks of activity ensued.

He had covered both possibilities.

Fifty Maurian WorkHouse Matists and thieves had been brought in, drugged, and injected with LifeCo Vuerven Extract.

Simultaneously, fourteen captured Vuervee had been injected with LifeCo Maurian Grade-One Extract.

Imagine. The Maurian mind and Heroic Integrity combined with the physical prowess of a Vuerve! The best of both.

The months of waiting, watching, noting . . .

And then, within four days of each other, both groups produced young.

From the Maurians who were injected with Vuerven Extract sprung all disappointments, totally Maurian in features—black hair, black eyes. They were the worst of both, dumb and slow, and only slightly slimmer. They were shipped to nurseries for maturing. That group, of which today only three males survived, had mostly died from weak immune systems. They all seemed to adapt, but showed no special features, save for extreme ordinariness.

Ahh, but the other group, he lamented . . . the Vuervee who were injected with Maurian Extract.

They were quite Vuerven in appearance—with some Maurian characteristics—and they had held the greatest hope for him, their creator. While they lived, Crilp's face beamed from every Corder. His name was on every Hero-minded Maurian tongue.

While they lived.

But with their deaths, mere 20Time apart, his life fell apart; and was blown away on the winds of failure.

Oh, he got along with whatever small priority assignments he could wrangle from an EnvirCo Mr. he had Black Materials on, but he was really just going through the motions.

Even now, with this last twitch of ambition, he knew he was shooting at a shadow. For what audience could he get, regardless of any Heroic discovery he might now make? In Mauria it was survival of the prominent, and he had vanished years ago.

Now in his fourth month of searching, searching for who knows what, he was tiring.

What went wrong with Project Hybrid? His chances for one successful Hybrid were collated to 94.86. Even after the failure, if he could have found just *one* scientist in Mauria who could understand his equations . . . surely another project would have been authorized.

But it was spelled out to him plain and cold: the public could not be reached again by his name. His idea. Plus (and he always suspected this was really behind it) MarPrex had just instigated a ten-year program to encourage the detesting of all Vuervee to compensate for public anomie of Maurian features. Thus, history combined with chance to destroy the rightful Hero of Maurian science. Even Vuerven Extract had been outlawed. Politics!

With bitterness in his motions, Mr. Scientist Crilp lit up the banks of collators for his 64th recollate in as many days. He sighed, and wondered why he was bothering.

Assumptions, he thought. Assumptions were poison to truth. Make no assumptions. Open the mind. See the data as a Corder would. Objectively. No values, no opinions, no expectations . . .

. . . and then it hit him like a clap of thunder.

* * * * * * * * * * * * * *

Suddenly, it was not so wonderful. Young Trebel shivered on the floor of her new cave-home. The fire was doing little to repell the wet cold from penetrating, and hunger gnawed.

She would give anything to be back in a warm, controlled room, with food. Even the rank WorkHouse Grell made her mouth drool.

As the day, and then night had come, she had collected reasons not to find food, not to hunt. She glanced to her tapered spear, leaning against a fire-colored rock. It scared her.

Tomorrow, she promised, tomorrow; and fell asleep. As the dry warmth of sleep covered her form, she wondered—oddly—of her mother. Who she was seemed important, now, though it was not to the Maurians.

It was not to her, but for this moment of hunger-weakened sleep.

* * * * * * * * * * * * * *

"Noooo! No!"

Mr. Scientist Crilp's midnight scream awoke his Lady from the main room. She crept in, blinking at the laboratory lights. Her legs swayed from sleepiness.

"Crilp," she asked, "what is it?"

"My Lady," this took much effort, "the Hybrid, the one Female—remember, she had the, uh, the green streak in her hair!"

"Wha—"

"Yes! It was her. It had to be! We just *assumed* that it had to be a *Male*! We ignored her."

"You know I don't understand these . . . "

"Grell and gruff," rambled the old scientist, his mind boiling, "we thought only a male could be the new Hero prototype. She was it, and she lives! The Hybrid! She lives! Even now! As I sit here an old man, my life's work lives the life of a CommonerGirl, somewhere in Mauria!"

His eyes were wide, eyebrows bowed in macabre appreciation of life's twists. He laughed, thinking how Maurian Heroes would react to the idea that a CommonerGirl was the next evolutionary step for the Maurian race.

"I'll fix you some hot drink."

"My Lady. Did you listen?"

"I heard." Lady Crilp's face was hard, sad. "How could a female be a Hero? Even if it was possible, who would believe you now? Who will even give you audience? And you were sure then, and you're sure now. The best is to drown the whole thing in a hot drink and let it alone. Please."

"I tell you with the rest of my spirit I will open the door. I will get my due. I will give you the life you are owed. I will game and trade and black reed my way to glory! You will yet be a Heroic Lady with Integrity."

"It matters not now. You will always be a Hero to me."

He walked, bowed with age, over to his Lady, looked upon her, and touched her brow in tenderness. "I'd enjoy a hot drink."

Lady Crilp's middle-black eyes glowed warm. Mr. Scientist Crilp smiled. Even as long as they'd been together, he still loved to be served by her.

Lady Crilp bundled her dated lace tunic about her as she shuffled away.

She was still loved.

CHAPTER ELEVEN
'Meadow Ring'

The day dawned cool, clear and folliage-crisp. The Sun beamed down on Mauria from a cloudless sky. Snow drifted about the Plains, save for the gleaming metallic square of Mauria, where night-cooled FareBeams screeched with SonaRails racing to work.

Even the gaming district looked clean, somehow of higher source than usual, under this windy new day.

Small gamer and ParlorMan Bordt couldn't remember laying eyes upon this Mr. before. New customer. Better slick up the manners. His missing tooth beckoned to the well-dressed old Mr.

"Good day, sir, what can the finest small gamer in the land do fer ya'? The name's Bordt, as in the name of the place!"

The eyes that turned to Bordt were those of a searcher. MarSek? This was no small gamer, at rate.

"My Hero, Bordt," the man began, and Bordt knew he was in need to address him so, "I was told that the art of gaming still flourishes effectively in your Parlor. From the highest opinion."

"Aye, sir, but there are hundreds of others as well, though I'm gratef . . . "

"Your modesty is as real as that vulgar sign above your door, Mr. Bordt; neverso, it is you I seek."

"Well put, but what could I possibly assist you with? I don't ever see ya before."

"What I need may be worth much to you—and please, just for

an old Mr., use pre-respected language. My name is unimportant at this time. Let's just say I'm in bad need of Black Materials for a high purpose. A profitable purpose for you. UniCopies, of course, certified UniCopies."

"Mr., begging your pardon, but you know all secrets are reported to MarSek, and I would . . . "

"Bordt, I am not a MarSekMan. When and if you achieve gamed materials for me, I will be honored to exhibit my identity, *before* you utter a clue as to their content."

"Just for me . . . my own curiosity, Mr., who would ye' be needing these materials on?"

"I'm glad we understand each other, Bordt. The targets are any member of the Control Council."

Bordt's face paled. "Di . . . did you say the Control Council?!"

"I did, Bordt. And perhaps 500,000Book will drain your face of that fright you've so admirably faked. Upon delivery, of course."

"Not that I can help, Mr. Sir, but if I should receive some interesting goods, where might I reach you?"

"At this number. Thank you for your time."

Mr. Scientist Crilp turned aristocratically and took leave of "Bordt's Exotic Trade and GamingParlor."

The moment his boots struck the grainy alloy of the FareWay he sighed relief. How sad. The fourteenth such place and no encouragement. As if to punctuate the wry mood of a Mr. Scientist flitting about gaming and trading parlors, his eye caught the SonaSign under Bordt's shop.

It was a crude likeness of a Mr. Sir being helped from his expensive looking SonaRail by an elegantly thin Lady. Ha! Fat chance in *this* district. Well, he should talk. He didn't have 500,000Book anymore than he had three legs! But, one had to be bold. . . especially at *his* age. How else to get audience for Project Hybrid . . . number two?

* * * * * * * * * * * * * * *

They must have entered her cave while she slept. For now they stood around her laughing. Taunting. How pleased they were now, thought young Trebel. Mr. Advisor Steen and all those other axiom-spewing controllers of the WorkHouse were floating around her.

"You see," they chortled, voices echoing about the cave, "this is all wrong. Like *everything* you've done. What are you going to Grell up *next*? Come back to *us*. You *need* us. *We* need *you*. *We'll* make you better."

Trebel shook on the cold floor, partly conscious. Now, as new Sun lanced pin-speckles on her nearly awakened face, Mr. Behaviorist Hairn danced into focus.

"Really, Trebel. This is a bit much, isn't it? This fire, this cave? Did those silly books go to your head? Just like that perverse Matist who you let filth up your life. That was just the beginning of a long list of dumb things, wasn't it, Trebel?"

Did you think Mating would be fun, too, like *this* book adventure? Did you? Did you? Did you? Did you?"

"Yes!!" Trebel relived her exasperated admission. "Curse you, yes. It was, yes, exciting. And so is this!"

Consciousness washed in, fading the images out. But the Behaviorist's pitying eyes remained a burn in her eye until she stumbled to the cave mouth, and the bright day flooded her thoughts clean.

Food.

The idea seared through her rumbling stomach. No more self pity. Action time. She grabbed her spear. The air felt good as she set off upon her hunt, the ground tickling her bare feet, the Sun kissing her skin.

Suddenly, she was back to Trebel of old, a cocky grin to the sky, a sauntered arrogance to the step. She visioned Mr.'s tending to her, enchanting her, ravishing her—must be the hunger—and she readied her eyes to spot the colorful hair of the Vuervee, salivating at the thought!

Dillon's blue hair faded from the melting snow, and now the hot Sun. Still he slept in this meadow. Within his dream, he stood upon a ridge of pebbles and sand. He stared upon a great mountain range, with one graceful peak jutting high above the others, its snow covered a proud crown.

Dillon told the mountain, "I am imperfect. I am wrong. You . . . are the tallest. You are perfect!"

The mountain spoke to Dillon:

"Look at my height! Now look at the sky, whose height I cannot see . . . whose height humbles the poor mound of *my* form! Yet I tower over my kind. I did not grow there, I wore away *slower* than the others. I resisted the elements *more* than the others. And so I am more exposed, and am worn away by the winds as I protect those below me."

And now the great peak raised its arms skyward and said, "Pity no form, hate no form, ask not of its being, for it is you!"

And now the mountain changed to Blisfur, and Blisfur's arms reached toward Dillon.

But a noise awakened Dillon from his sleep.

Blisfur's image lingered, a filmy shadow reaching to Dillon as his eyes focused on something new: A ring of Maurians, guns aimed to his head.

He blinked, but they were real. So, I am to End, then.

He tensed, awaiting the all too familiar beep of the guns, the water-smooth entry of darts. So this was it. Finally. His Sign. He was to End in a Circle of uniformed Maurians.

He stared at them, waiting for it.

Mud had caked Trebel's limbs. She cowered under a prickly bush, breath choked for fear of discovery.

It was soon after leaving her cave that a blue flash of forehair caught her sight. Spear poised, she had crept towards it. From a short distance, she hesitated, not fully understanding a Vuerve sleeping in the middle of an open meadow.

The extra moments of thought saved her. For another noise soon scurried her into this bush, scratching her badly, but not badly enough to return to the WorkHouse. Soon there appeared a band of MarSekMen, oddly dressed for a hunting party.

Instead of the usual bright tunics they practically camouflaged. Instead of military cry and cadenced march, it was stealthy creep, until the sleeping Vuerve with liquid blue color was completely encircled.

It was brave, this one. It just waited for it. Staring at them. A look of disdain radiated through its handsome features. Shoot it, already, you low ruts!

But now, very stiffly, a Maurian dressed with officer's ForeBar walked to Dillon and spoke thusly:

"The Maurian Controllers respectfully request a meeting with the people of Vuerve."

A document was handed to Dillon, and forty armed Maurians awaited his reply. Before he answered, many moments went by.

"I will carry the message." Dillon looked at the document on thin alloy. "But we do not understand these markings."

A few Maurians held back smirks. It was another of Fruke's PR thrusts—put the animals off-balance from the start.

"What," asked Dillon, "does it say?"

"It says there will be a meeting."

"You have said this."

"Do not game with me, Anim . . . , look. These men here," he swept on his boots to the MarSek troupe, "are your friends."

"All are," said Dillon.

Now he turned to Dillon, a forced smile etched into his craggy face.

"In any case, Vuerve, make a mark upon the message, and return it to me. The meeting will be on your soil, right here in this open meadow. We reserve the right of Corders and the presence of our press. We bring only defense SonaGuns. The meeting will be the day after next."

The Maurian took a breath, and forced CounterFlow . . .

"Our Controllers s-send their l-love. The meeting will be promptly at 500Time, uh, Sun is straight up. Do you accept?"

"For myself, yes. I will tell the message to the Vuervee." The Maurians trod away, leaving Dillon to Ment to this amazing overture.

He had asked for a Sign, and it had come. Dillon's mind reeled with confusion. Rare was the Sign without mystery, but rare was a mystery such as this! It was all there, somewhere. The Maurians forming the sacred Circle about him . . . Blisfur.

And that strange Maurian girl hiding in the Prickly bush, even now silent.

Dillon disappeared into a nearby stand of woods, and was valleys away before any more noises were heard in this small clearing.

Young Trebel cursed and began painfully extracting herself from the barbs. Even now, out here, the Maurians *would* find a way to keep PrimeVuerve from her belly!

* * * * * * * * * * * * * *

Duerr squatted in a lush valley of spring growth. His soul was happy past wildest hopes. That his Circle would be crowned by such a loving brood of young! He Mented to the celebration of Spring budding about him. A group of young, only a season older than his own newborn, bounced and played nearby.

He heard barefoot steps running over a small rise near the young. He turned to see a strange Maurian girl cant down the hill, spear poised in the air as she ran at the young.

Dear Circle! She was a hunter?!

Young Trebel had scrambled through canyon and over ridge. She was angry, hungry and growing desperate. The hunger pangs rumbled again and Trebel moaned in pain and fear. What would happen to her? This was no fun, this book adventure.

But ho-de-hi! Look there! She spotted a colorful group of young Vuervee below her! Her mouth watered. The luck, it had changed! Not even high Mr. Sirs dined on young Vuervee but for special occasions!

She charged.

The Vuervee jumped to their feet scrambling to escape. All managed but green and yellow Diar, who caught his foot in a noose of plant chutes.

He was all but cooked, reveled Trebel!

But suddenly, leaping into her path was the rusty-red blur of an adult Vuerve.

Grell, she cursed. This one-armed animal was freeing the young one, and she would not get close enough for a throw at either of them Unless . . . she drew the spear back and heaved with all her frustration.

Duerr used his reed to slit the viney tentacles from young Diar's foot, pulling him free of the tangled growth.

But now there was a sudden warmth, as the point of a spear slipped into Duerr's back.

He pushed Diar ahead of him to scurry away, then locked his hand around the lance behind him, so it could not be pulled from him and used on the fleeing young.

The ground tilted.

He fell.

Young Trebel, mouth awash in triumph, bounced to the groaning Duerr. This was fantastic! Her first kill!

But . . . he was still moving . . . and the blood.

Her eyes widened, and she swallowed hard, hands limp at her side, body bowed forward. Her throat was suddenly bone-dry. She gagged.

"Are you proud?" asked Duerr with dimming voice.

Trebel screamed. This wasn't the way it happened! No. You hunted, and they fell over. Then they became neatly piled blocs of bronzed meat to trim and grind. Not all this blood! And that hideous spear standing straight up, stuck in this form who *spoke* to her.

Trebel sunk to the ground.

"Are you going to eat me, little girl?" Only Duerr's mouth moved, feeling had left his body.

"I—I'm hungry. It was, it was you or me."

"So you chose me." A gasp of pain.

"Well, of . . . of course." Trebel began to cry. "I . . . didn't know, I . . . I thought . . . "

And now Trebel sobbed, for even her book adventure had turned out wrong.

"I'm . . . I'm so sorry, I didn't . . . I was so hungry."

Within his pain, his fading senses, Duerr Mented to this Maurian who wept.

"Little girl . . . " but the pain stopped any further words.

Trebel's eyes stared quietly, her form was still.

Duerr fought to release his last thought. "If there is one Maurian who cries . . . ugh . . . a new beginning . . . the End is the beginning . . . leave me here. I am warm.

"Eat . . . ungh! Eat the blue and yellow berries, cook . . . augh! Cook the cones, not the middle. Find the . . . roots of the Mindo plant, blue flowers, yellow leaves. Eat them . . . without fire. Take . . . the . . . "

And Duerr Ended.

His craggy face was still and peaceful. Above, a small white cloud skimmed over the low Sun.

The wind was still.

For long, Trebel lay with him, cradling his head, stroking his auburn forehair.

They were two still figures draped upon a forest floor, night spreading through the Spring buds.

CHAPTER TWELVE
'The Gaming Begins'

Mr. Granes' living quarters were messy from at least three previous meals, and more than one friend's visit for SourDrink and a game of Terrain. On the wall by his dressing table, all of his LifeCo Extract bids approved by Mr. Sir Burn for actual contracts hung in burnished frame. Unfortunately for Granes, this still left much wall to be decorated. Like most middle-Misters in the reproduction industry, Granes was single. Dealing with Extract day after day gave one a funny view of family: one waited till one could really afford the best. Fine Extract was like fine, aged SourDrink, you didn't rush it.

Granes watched the day's events on his Corder, shifting irritably in his web-metal swinging chair. He flipped the Corder off. Boring. What was needed was a Maurian FieldDay! Just the thought of hundreds of Maurians swarming through the hills . . .

All this killer-Vuervee talk. Some idiot had probably lost his tube and suffocated to death! Bunch of fools. If I were Blench, and not a lousy 54th Mr., I'd get a new MarPrex man who could handle fairy tales!

His Box beeped.

"Hello? . . . Bordt?! How did you get my inter-number?"

"Day to ya', Mr. Granes. I'll be brief, not wantin' to stir ye' at home. I have a certain . . . trader, whose interested in purchasing materials. I thought of you first, sir."

"First. Grell! I'm at least 200th on any list you care to name,

Bordt. Although I'm probably first on *yours* after all you've gamed out of me!"

"These materials must be concerning a member of the . . . Control Council."

"Oh. Well, if I hear anything I'll let you know," Granes said off-hand.

Bells clanged and buzzed in Bordt's head. Granes had not ridiculed the proposal, as the scores of others he had Corded. Moreso, his reply was unnaturally matter-of-fact. Granes' clumsy CounterFlow was a bright red flag.

"I understand." Bordt's voice was calm, verging on disinterest. "Your materials will serve you best. It's just that every high Mr. Sir, Mr. Granes, as yer know well, bought his way there at one time or another."

"True enough, Bordt, but even if I had something on Mr. Sir Councillor Blench himself, he could only buy it with favor. An unaccounted 1OBook is enough for a scandal that high up. You know that."

"Ah, but ye've overlooked those down a bit lower, who are not watched so close. What could yer do with . . . 400,000Book, Mr. Granes?"

Granes felt his lungs contract. 400,000Book! Whatever favors he could hold Rute for, they couldn't top what *that* sort of power could wield.

"You must be joking. One could just about buy his way to the Control Council itself."

"Yes, *you* could, couldn't you?"

"Surely, you are joking . . . or gaming."

"Always gaming, never joking. A fat Book is no laughing matter. See you tomorrow at 600Time?"

"Perhaps. Perhaps."

"Oh, Mr. Granes, one small detail, if you don't mind. Eh, there's a matter of timing involved. My trader may take his BookCredits elsewhere if I don't . . . keep his interest."

"So?"

"So if you *did* have any materials . . . "

"I've told you . . . "

"Yes, I know. It's just that 400,000Book doesn't come along every day, anyso. Mr. *Sir* Granes, just off the rail: *who* is your favorite Hero on the Council?"

Silence.

Granes' mind raced. Bordt was asking for a hard signal, to know if Granes' was just dolly-wagging or not. What to do, he thought? Why tip off Bordt that there were Black Materials, or who they were on?

Then again, this could be the moment to play his main Terrain Piece. With *those* kind of BookCredits, Granes could leap to Council heights without waiting for Rute to ascend.

And what if Rute never made it, he considered? Maybe this crazy Vuerven meeting would work for Blench, and Rute's bid would be quelled. Maybe Rute would be out completely, then what would his Black Materials be worth?

This might be a *sure* way up. He didn't want Bordt to look elsewhere, yet . . . .

"Are you there," Bordt's voice raked?

"1Time, Bordt. I'm . . . thinking."

Granes gritted his teeth. Whatso, he thought, this might be the time for his grand Array. Here he was *still* just a middle Mr.

But he still felt deadlocked. His only Materials . . . his one chance for high Integritorial Heroship . . .

Heroes had risen on a lot less. You wait, you sit, . . . you lose. As he always had.

Go ahead . . .

"My favorite Hero?" said Granes. "Why that would be Mr. Sir. Engineer Rute, of EnvirCo. Quite a Hero."

* * * * * * * * * * * * * *

Mr. Sir Rute paced nervously. Lady Rute and their son, a 7th-Level student, were to meet him 20Time ago. His large lips pursed in frowning disapproval. This scowl was more his birthmark, everso, than his attitude. He wore it no matter the mood. It was in this downturned mouth where the harsh memories, the years of struggle, the effort to break his modest Extract, had settled.

His Corder rung.

"Yes?"

"Mr. Engineer Rute, Sir?"

"Yes. Who is this?" Rute asked.

"No matter, Mr. Sir. It's just that I'll be in middle touch with certain Black Materials over you, Mr. Sir, and wondered if you'd care to make a bid."

Well, considered Rute, *that* is certainly to the point.

"I'll double any bid. Just tell me where and when. And make certain with your life they're UniCopies."

"Very good, Mr. Sir. A light test is yours upon inspection. The bid I already have is 500,000Book."

"What?! You know I can't . . . " Mr. Sir Rute hesitated, then recovered. "Yes, . . . uh, yes I will double that bid. When and Where?"

"I'll re-contact you," said Bordt, and the Corder went dead.

So, thought Rute, Granes had shown his ugly head! That amount of BookCredits was, naturally, out of the question; but . . . there were many pieces on a Terrain board.

To be sure, Rute was happy and relieved that he would finally have his shot at Granes' materials—at this unceasing sore upon his life.

It could be worse, he thought. Granes could have simply sold them to another. Then some other rotten Grell would bleed him for who knows how long.

He wondered who the voice on the phone was.

* * * * * * * * * * * * *

FareWay 141N had seen much noteworthy activities this day. The very FareWay itself was forged from conflicting character. There was a time not long ago when all of the FareWay, from InterFare 37E to InterFare 79W, was a solid ribbon of independent contractors, Recreation Parlors, and a patchwork of small gaming places.

It now stood a confused, abstract defenseline. As the plight of the independent worsened, more and more of the old Parlors displayed the bright red logo of Family Industries. So it was not surprising that this embattled FareWay reflected its mixed Integrity.

For example, over at InterFares 141N-25W, the 126th petty Mating of the season occurred when a beam-maintenance assistant and a ParlorGirl were overcome with criminal passion. A passing Mr. Sir had reported it on his Corder. The MarSekMan had fined the maintenance assistant on the spot—140Book—and sped the girl off to the WorkHouse.

At InterFare 141N-35E, a Mr. of EnvirCo had lost a brawl of insults to a small gamer, and began to cry in full view of anyone who cared to turn their eye and ear.

At InterFare 141N-87W, a Family Industries' secret contractor had outgamed a struggling ParlorMan for 15,000Book.

Within 20Time, an appraisor from MarSupply had acquired the Parlor for Family Industries.

And now, CityMauria in deep dusk, the surrounding Plains a flat black, only one Parlor on 141N burnt a lamp past closing time.

Two shadowed forms hulked over a table in low discussion:

"There is no question as to your faithfulness, or mine, Mr. Granes. It's just that I want *you* to be satisfied."

Bordt and Mr. Granes eyed each other, two silhouettes in Bordt's musty Parlor.

Bordt continued. "To insure your trust, I am giving you the license to my Parlor. Me life. It's all I have. If I am dishonest, you have that. Since I have no other skill, you would be holding the key to my survival. The license can be verified by any means you desire."

Mr. Granes had not forgotten the other times he thought he had control of Bordt. But on those occasions, he speculated, Bordt would either lose or win. Simple gaming. In this case, they would *both* win. Anyso, it was difficult for Mr. Granes to see through the dollydreams:

Visions of leaning back in Hero's armchair, pondering an issue before the Control Council, glancing around the table at the other Heroes of Mauria. Such, and more, danced before Mr. Granes.

"Just so you know, Bordt, that I'll be watching for any albino actions on your part. And you'll be very, very sorry if there is the least blotch on your Integrity."

"Mr. Granes, Sir, my gaming days will be over, thanks to the fee for placing your Materials. And *your* Mr. days are numbered, Mr. Sir! I'm pleased to have brought you to the right market place for your goods. I am only interested in my BookCredit fee for bringing a buyer and seller together. It will be enough for my retirement."

Mr. Granes and Bordt each shared a measured grin, and nodded agreement. They stood up, stiff and tired from the long and concentrated CounterFlow, and there was no more to say.

As Granes pushed through the portal and sliced into the night, Bordt reached for his Corder and began to press numbers.

* * * * * * * * * * * * * * *

Mr. Scientist Crilp had spent the last day and a half tirelessly pouring through the files at schools and MarSek centers, chasing endless leads.

She was named "Treb," but the trail ended there, too many years back for Crilp's limited access.

Moreso, his plan to raise Black Materials on a high Hero now seems to have faded with everything else. Not one call had rewarded his degrading tour of gamers and other unsavory corners of Integritorial Mauria.

Ho, it had been half of a joke, anyso. A wild dart. 500,000Book!

His audacity amazed him. What would he have done if someone actually *had* Black Materials on a Control Councillor and took him up on his offer?

His Corder beeped. Whatso? He answered. "Yes?"

"Eh, Mr., Sir?"

"Who is this?"

"One of the, uh, gentleman you visited about certain . . . "

"Yes, yes. You've found something?"

"Well," said Bordt with convincing weariness, "I've had me ear to all places and people, if yer follow, Sir, and I thought I'd give yer the courtesy of tellin' you there's just no such a thing as you be seeking."

"Oh. Oh, I see," said Crilp." Well, things go as they do."

"And not just that, Sir," Bordt's voice hushed a bit, "there were some MarSekMen here a bit back—probably as a result of me inquries—asking who wanted these . . . materials."

"Oh, no! Did you give them my number?" The old scientist's heart began to pound.

"Well, Mr. Sir, I didn't, and won't since ye came to me as an honest gamer . . . "

"Well, I . . . don't know how to thank you . . . "

"Bother yourself not about that, Sir, but do me the favor of stopping your little . . . search, *you* know, so no more heat blows my way? "

"Done, consider it done! And thank you!"

The two rang off. Crilp, still red-faced with embarrassment, sighed his relief. Old fool, he thought. How about a nice stint in the WorkHouse to ease your retirement? He would be more careful. Try another direction.

Something in the old scientist just wouldn't quit.

I will find you, Treb. I will find my Hybrid.

* * * * * * * * * * * * *

"Good evening, Maurians and Heroes."

Mr. Sir Rute's console blared through his dinner. He ate quickly, nervously. "Here's the grand happenings in dynamic Mauria today . . ."

Rute's mind had been tightroping an anxiety wire since the call from the anonymous gamer. So Granes had finally made his move. Good. The persistent drag of not being in full control was even this moment souring a spread-steak of Prime Southern Vuervee.

He and Lady Rute sat in elegant Maurian dinner tunics, knifing through the Prime meat, tenderly poking little square chunks into their mouths, their webbed alloy bibs sparkling over the shiny plates.

About them, all styles of decor graced the room. Four Ladies had, after all, added their touches. The new Lady Rute had a stomach disorder, and were it not for this incredibly tender Prime Rute had cajoled from Bard at MarSupply, she would be resigned to Medical Mix.

This was one Lady grateful for her Hero's lofty position. He glanced idly across her young beauty. She always wore tunics which revealed the lines of her stout chest and thighs. When the slightest worry settled on his mind, he would watch her elegance, and problems danced away.

The Console blared its baritone excitements. "The meeting with the Vuervee of the hills takes place tomorrow, and what a grand moment! The mysterious killer Vuervee are expected to be turned over to Maurian authorities with grandiose apologies. Mr. Sir Engineer Rute himself stated in an exclusive interview with . . ."

Ah. Fruke came through. His own voice on the Console asided his attention: " . . . that a great civilization as ours can and *will* modify forces of destruction, be they from above or below, from within or without, or from . . . *the dark caves of the past*," he mouthed with the broadcast. Not bad. Especially that view of him standing with the Sun turning his hair silver. Nice touch.

His Corder rang, automatically muting the sound from the news.

"Yes?" he answered. "Yes, I have the BookCredits. Of course. I'll be there. . . . Bordt's your name, I've got it, fine. Just you there, now, alone. . . . All right. After the Vuerve meeting, you understand. Yes, good-bye."

"My Lady," he began, "I am going to rid Mauria of one fool, and put another into my undying service. Fix us a celebration drink. SernicSour, I believe!"

"Yes, my Hero."

But Lady Rute had never heard her calm, studious, Engineer Hero speak with such . . . flair and fire.

It worried her.

CHAPTER THIRTEEN
'The Portal of Truth'

Tedrin sensed someone near. He had been Menting to many mysteries: Brinta and Dillon's strange vanishing, the lack of Maurians in the hills. In the past, this had meant a hunting slaughter—the Maurians called it a FieldDay.

Why did he, the loved and trusted VeemVa, not move his Vuervee farther into the hills, further from the hunters?

Why did he squat in his Womb, staring bleakly at the portal? He had waited for a Sign, and that was why.

And there was a dark form, nearby.

"Tedrin."

"Dillon?"

"Yes."

"Tell it to Dillon, or Hiola, or Venes. And you will know which to tell, for one will enter this same Womb as did Kurk, on another day of great confusion for you . . ."

Blisfur's words drained the stiffness from Tedrin, and he knew now why he has kept his Veem in this place, next to the warm-spring river. It was the very water where Dillon's father—the Maurian Kurk—Ended.

Dillon entered Tedrin's womb. In this dark shelter, he noticed that the Moon reflected many aged layers of needles and branches. Tedrin forgets to change valleys, he thought. Tedrin's features appeared to be fading in the dim light of the womb. His red, moon-streak melted to brown, brown forehair showed strips of white and yellow.

"Tedrin . . . I have broken the Circle!"

"That a friend of mine would claim such strength," smiled Tedrin, "gives hope to all!"

Dillon frowned at Tedrin's sad smile.

The VeemVa's face glowed tenderness and pity for Dillon. "The Circle cannot be, if it can be broken. But speak."

"I've Ended another's life! A Maurian. I . . . have killed!"

For long, Tedrin bowed his head. Dillon's eyes pierced to the older Blisfur's son, but Tedrin's face seemed relieved. Dillon wondered how this could be of telling him what no Vuerve can do!

"Shows of their true self, does it not?" Tedrin smiled. "A Vuerve Ends a hunter; and they run from the hills, guns and all."

"How can you be so calm?" Dillon demanded. "Did you hear what I said?"

"What is, is beautiful. We can make no ugliness, but for our own water views, what we *think* we see. You have killed. I grieve for your thoughts. The ugliness is in your vision of this deed. You try to make this what it cannot be. I cannot tell you why this was to happen, or why it is of beauty.

"Only that it *must* be, . . . for it is. Now, Dillon, you will know what only I know. If you have killed, it is we who have killed, through you."

"Your words confuse me," said Dillon.

Tedrin's eyes were sadder than Dillon had ever seen them, and he reached his hand to Dillon.

Dillon clutched it, and held firm. His eyes reflected Tedrin's, which reflected Dillon's.

"I do not know of the full truth, dear brother and friend," Tedrin began. "You must search, and learn: and find a place for this storm in your sunny days which must dawn.

"I will tell you now: You are not only of Vuerven blood. Of your mother, she was Blisfur, as was mine. But of your father, his name was Kurk, a Maurian. Lover of Blisfur. It is so. You, Hiola, and Venes are fruit of Kurk and Blisfur, late in her Circle."

Dillon's throat held these words and choked his voice quiet. His deep blue eyes sank below lids as he swallowed this shock.

The shadows changed, and changed again.

The wind rose, then slowly quieted.

The Moon dropped behind a Cuervo.

And, at last, Dillon found slow words.

"I have always known this deep within. But, whatever the seed, be there Maurian blood within me . . . I must . . . be Ended."

Tedrin squeezed Dillon's limp, icy palm.

"My mother's blood also flows within you, *your* mother," Tedrin said. "It is not for you to End that. The great Circle makes no demands on us, other than to live its truth.

"You are here. Thereof, you have a purpose in the Circle. I see you turning yourself inside, making much of yourself, little of yourself, help of yourself, hurting yourself, searching yourself.

"Instead, go forth and out to help—and hurt—the Circle. Live! That someday you see a Veem flourish from your guiding path, that someday you love the flower as the fallen tree, the prickly Dura as the Goldenleaf; I beg you to raise your leaves to the Sun.

"Whatever reason of your deed, it is good or for learning, as all things are. The ugliness, as you well know, is what *you* see, not *what* you see!

"Long I have guided Venes, long I have guided Hiola. Yet have I found a Va to continue the great Circle of Ganfer's Veem, Blisfur's Veem. Tedrin's Veem.

"Long I have watched you, knowing you are him. I know of your fear, your blinded eye, your pain. And your beauty. I ask *help*! Not sadness, not happiness. Only your help."

Dillon reached to Tedrin, and the two embraced. For long they remained so, Dillon asking strength from another for the last time.

And Tedrin felt the pulse within Dillon.

Tedrin felt old. He felt sad.

He felt peace.

On the third try, young Trebel was able to keep the handful of Cone seeds down. She blinked her eyes, swallowed again, and still the dour-tasting petals remained in her stomach. Success!

Her eye swung to the patch of ground carpet where she had buried Duerr. She chose a spot below a crest of hanging blue bonflowers. It had all been a tender nightmare, but finally she had placed the final clump of ground over his form.

Now she rubbed the colorful nut she removed from his neck. It was harder than rock, small, and she could hear some liquid inside. In Mauria, they were priceless wall items, but naturally she had never had one. Oddly she felt a comfort from Duerr's Birthgem, as if the Vuerve remained with her, a living presence, while his form rested beneath the flowers.

Her hunger continued, stronger than her repulsion for swallowing plants.

"Animal!" she heard Mauria scream at her. "Animal!"

Finally she had eaten enough to feel full for the first since escaping CityMauria.

Her spirit, still in shock, lifted enough for her to take a walk. As she passed through the bright, new foliage; over bushes and under tall, straight Cuervo trees; the fragrance of the budding Spring flowers delighted her—even through her tube.

The warm Sun lulled her senses to calm. The soft grass under her feet played with her spirit, and the array of surrounding colors sang to her eye. She was . . . happy, again. Almost.

She came to a rippling spring and followed it, humming a tune to match the water's own scale. Soon the brook met with a larger stream and formed a pool. She had lost all track of time and direction.

An impish grin splashed on her face, and now she sloshed around in the icy water. How cold it was! But soon she adjusted, and gasps of delight echoed from the high rock formations surrounding the pool.

This was everything she had dreamed of! And when she climbed from the water and rested to dry upon a smooth water-curved rock, the Sun's tingling rays warmed her to sleep, and the forest sang its song of Spring.

* * * * * * * * * * * * *

Dillon and Tedrin ate a smooth mash of Luma bulbs and sipped water from the warm-spring. They sat, feet in the water, staring at a proud bluff of rock and Whitebark stand.

"Many changes, Tedrin," said Dillon. "Brinta, she was Ended by the Maurians. I . . . Mated to her. I was angry, like never before! I squeezed the hunter's neck. And the rest ran . . . like we do from them. But I was sick from this deed and I wandered for long, looking for a Sign.

"Then I fell asleep in a meadow, and awoke to see a Circle—a sacred ring—of *Maurians* surrounding me! They were dressed in green, and all had guns aimed to my head.

"I have found my Sign, I thought. I will End. But then! One walked to me and said the Maurians want to meet us. Tomorrow, when the Sun is high! *Meet* with us!"

"I was young," Tedrin remembered, "when the last such meeting was. There was a group of friends called 'misters' who tried to explain how we needed each other—but that they had to keep the Vuervee at a 'level,' like a stream. They asked our help in knowing the size of us, so they could Ment to what they called 'kwotes.'

"There was no Menting of each other. They asked if we could tell them a number. 'Our size?' Ganfer said? Then he told them as best he could: 'Many to streams, few to trees'. We never thought to tell them we all were there! They became very angry. We felt sad at their anger, and offered play, food, gifts; but their Va said no, and thanked us of coming. That was."

"And the next Sun found many Maurians blacking the hills with hunting party. A FieldDay, it was, and many friends Ended.

"Dillon, "Tedrin said softly, "it must be of the Circle for *you* to be our guide at this meeting. It may be your Maurian blood which will let you reach them with words, where others of us could not. The Circle is."

＊＊＊＊＊＊＊＊＊＊＊＊＊＊

As Trebel slept upon this soft rock, a gentle breeze rustling the greening buds, her tube continued to drain of CO_2; and still she slept deeper than the pool beside her.

A low, alarming "pffft" woke her as the last of her air escaped.

Young Trebel bolted upright, gasping for breath.

My tube!

She scrambled to her feet, swaying dizzily, and then staggered towards her cave. As Oxygen poisoning became worse, each step was more effort; and now the trees and clouds stretched and swayed like they were made of hot EndoFirm.

Worse, she had to climb uphill, along the stream. Her chest was inflamed, she knew it was no use.

Must start . . . a fire. CO_2. Yes . . . a fire . . . how? Get some wood . . . no dry wood around . . . still damp . . . here . . . pile these . . . anyso . . . make a nice little triangle . . . yes, how pretty . . . all the branches . . . coming to a point . . . a point . . . now to start it . . . with . . . with . . . with . . .

Trebel collapsed to the ground.

Her lungs heaved and gagged on the Oxygen. Her feet and arms flailed grotesquely.

Finally, she was still.

CHAPTER FOURTEEN
'The Meeting'

A proud and gigantic Cuervo tree stood to the side of the large grassy meadow in which Dillon had been surrounded by Maurians. It had no leaf, and few branches. It had Ended long ago.

Yet it stood.

At Sunset, this largest of Needle trees threw its shadow from beneath its wise old trunk to the far side of the field. Every Spring, though, it aimed its black line directly at Mauria.

A hearty wind often swayed and creaked its enormous form to the very edge of upheaving its massive, unfeeling roots.

To the Vuervee, the tree was a center of Signs.

Many times Tedrin had Mented to the line of this tree that he might sense the ways of Mauria.

The Vuervee named the tree Boleurr.

The Vuervee believed they spoke to Ended friends through Boleurr.

Dillon had Mented to Boleurr of age. For long he would lean his head to the decaying bark, and learned of growing old. And learned of the aging of the Circle, and aging of the line.

Duerr had Mented to Boleurr's shadow, learning as a young Vuervee of the motion of changes. He could not see the shadow move, yet by turning away for a while, the shadow could be seen to have moved. Thus, he visioned, all change of the Circle hides its motion, but for later, looking back.

Ganfer, first mate to Blisfur, and VeemVa before her, had once taught Ended Duerr of the Maurians, who made marks upon the meadow, giving names to each mark. The mark the shadow was nearest was be the name of Changes.

The Maurians called this "time," as if the shadow jumped from place to place. This, Ganfer told, was Menting of the line. Menting of the Circle searched but for the motion, though it could not be seen.

Ganfer had told Duerr that Maurians spent much of life marking the line, and thus never saw the Circle together. Ganfer and Blisfur had Mated beneath Boleurr so that Tedrin, Sereoul and Colia were begun.

Now Boleurr stood over the meeting place of Vuervee and Maurians later this day. A brisk Spring wind fluttered and waved the grassy meadow. Boleurr's shadow speared to the heart of Tedrin's Veem, and by late sun it would aim its untouchable darkness to the grayish outline of Mauria, down below on the Plain.

And a great tired creak echoed from the bowels of the monster's trunk, punctuating the new day.

And then a louder crack was heard, as it let go.

****

A giant behemoth fashioned of luminous-bright alloy crunched, grinded, geared and shrieked across the EdgeHills, leaving a wake of trampled grass, crushed rock and pummelled branch.

The brightly finished monster exploded with reflections of the morning Sun, as its circular, alloy treads creaked and groaned towards the meeting meadow; carrying over 200 Maurians within. It was called a SonaGate.

In the rear of the vehicle was a brightly lit room with transparent maps, large rows of CompBoxes, charts, counters, Corders and screens; which projected four views of the passing terrain.

The SilverForm Wig set perfectly atop his head, Mr. Sir Councillor Blench spoke in low tones with the head of Mauria's military and security, MarSek's Mr. Sir Dunt. They confered quietly, that the technicians manning the various equipment did not hear, for Blench had become wary of anyone but Dunt, what with recent events which had shaken his empire.

"One more time, Dunt," declared Blench. "When my speech reaches the part about our willingness to . . . "

"Help the Vuervee to produce more plant-food," Dunt finished, annoyed at having to repeat again this simple plan, "my MarSekMen attack the Vuervee and wipe out at least 40 of them. Eh?"

"But you must give the signal to cut the Corders so Mauria doesn't see the attack! They must not see the Vuervee unarmed. How many times . . . "

"I know that, Blench, do you think me . . . "

"Okay, okay, Dunt. Just re-checking."

Blench's tall, dignified stoop paced and fidgeted next to Dunt's muscled trim; his thin face of concern twitched with thought as Dunt's square-jawed military face was calm, ready for battle. Blench's voice sped up.

"And since we know well," Blench's eyes seared Dunt's for any sign of uncertainty, "that *all* the Vuervee—local anyway—will, uh, come to the meeting, it shouldn't be any problem. Right?"

Dunt caught the note of insecurity in Blench's demeanor. He wondered if there wasn't something in that new Rute-Fruke bloc everyone whispered about.

"No problem. My MarSekMen will be upon them and shooting before they know anything."

Blench pursed his mouth, a hint of a smile playing upon the dark red lips. "Ring of killer-Vuervee slain!" Blench could taste the viewcasts now, the power-structure back to stability. Instead of Rute and Fruke eroding his PR and lit up as successors-to-be, it would be the re-success of Blench, with Dunt aside to the wings.

Even Fruke would see he was playing his power too early, and jump aboard the revived Blench machine, which would then crush him and Rute, naturally, like this SonaGate crushed the grass!

Yes, thought Mr. Sir Councillor Blench, life was a scintillating challenge. A creative concern.

* * * * * * * * * * * * * *

The SonaGate ground and chopped relentlessly, if slowly, through the EdgeHills. Massive sides of alloy blinded the hills with flares of shimmering reflections, as the mammoth bus bounced closer.

The 200 riders, and the uncountable weight of equipment, were frequently bumped uncomfortably, temporarily disrupting games of Kurl, Restriction and Terrain; spilling SourDrinks.

In the meeting meadow, up ahead, the technicians were already unloading wires from a smaller bus, carefully hiding visual, audio, and communi wires in every available bush, and even through the fallen trunk of a very old, large tree. This recently fallen giant was too large to move before meeting time.

Back in the belly of the monstrous terrain vehicle, Mr. Sir Councillor Blench now entertained MarPrex media by answering questions:

"What exactly are the Vuervee expecting in return for delivering this group of killers?"

"How did they contact you?"

"What will the punishment be?"

"Why won't there be any wires at the secret discussion table?"

Well, nodded Blench, Fruke had at least fed the reporters the right information. He smiled, held up a hand.

"Please, please. The representatives of the government of Vuerve want nothing in return. They realize the balance must be maintained. They don't want killers among them, either. Punishment will be justly tried by our great Legal Council, and the reason no sound will come from the meeting table is because . . . *that* was the *only* way the Vuervee would meet with us."

"Who is their representative?"

"How have they captured these killers?"

"Who will be . . . "

* * * * * * * * * * * * * *

Tedrin, Venes, Hiola and Dillon stepped quickly—Vuerven quiet—through the forest. The Sun was near high, and there was much worry on Tedrin's brow. Since Bobber's wails of anguish late last night told all of Duerr's Ending, Tedrin had chosen to see this meadow with his young brothers, before bringing the whole Veem.

It was passed on, that of long before, the Maurians have spoken one way and done another. Part of their Circle was hidden from view, he thought.

They heard the voices and equipment sounds long before they approached the meeting place.

When they reached the edge of the meadow, some Maurians were seen putting long strands in the ground.

But as they crouched into the first waving blades of meadow grass, all but Venes came to a stiff halt, eyes narrowing, mouths parted, minds frozen.

For there, next to its shadow, lay the fallen corpse of the great Needletree Boleurr.

Bark which clung even past leaves now cluttered the Spring green grass with decayed bits. The once giant tree rested—cracked in half—and first ever in middle Sun, pointed directly to Mauria.

Tedrin held a restraining arm to Venes' impatiently raised forehair as he, Dillon and Hiola Mented to this Sign. The Maurian entourage did not see them.

Venes had trouble Menting. The shiny, decorated tunics of the

Maurians fascinated him, as ever, and were dangling jewels blocking his tunnel of concentration.

"Duerr," began Dillon, "and now Boleurr. I weep for the great learning trunk, now crumbled and Ended past End. But a tree so great does not crumble for a breeze. Nor does a Duerr. Were I of my own Veem, Tedrin, I would ask to not gather with the Maurians this day."

Tedrin knew Dillon was right, even as his own Menting found but a confusing blur without Sign.

"I have ever known," said Hiola, "to keep away from the Maurians. Perhaps now, Tedrin, you will hear *my* words!"

"I say," Venes declared with raised whisper, "that this means no such thought! I feel a new day. A way of *thinking*, rather than dreaming. With this tree, our old ways crumble, and we grow to a new forest. A new way!"

"That being?" asked Tedrin, fully known that Venes had not Mented to the tree.

"That being a Vuerven and Maurian coming together. This day, at this meeting. I Ment of good, less fear for us, and . . . uh. . a new day. Tedrin, you speak of future, perhaps of *my* Veem. I feel this day can go far to ending Maurian murder! And this concerns me for Suns yet to rise."

Dillon saw the hurt anger in Tedrin's face, and said, "Venes, you do not Ment to the tree."

"That my wrongness," spat Venes, "would serve your own hopes of being VeemVa, Dillon."

"That is my last want, brother. A Va does not seek to lead. The Circle makes such choices. But if you seek the way to Va upon a line, here is some branch for your fire: I have killed—Ended another's life. I killed one who does not see the Circle, but one who is of it."

Venes frowned, oddly unshaken by Dillon's confession.

"Dillon. This is wrong." Tedrin spoke calmly. "Venes totters. Do not tempt him to follow the line, unless you are willing to follow after him."

Dillon's eyes softened, and he stepped to Venes and hugged him hard. Venes returned this hug, but not all of it.

"We have both lost the Circle, brother," Venes said, and his voice echoed between Tedrin and Dillon like a hollow nut bouncing in a rocky gorge.

The staunch Hiola turned away, eager to leave the Maurians; eager to leave the unVuerven speakings of the line. He would not be pulled into Maurian-like conflict! He knew the next VeemVa could only be he, Hiola, whose roots waivered not from the Circle.

Quietly, the group slid into the forest.

* * * * * * * * * * * * * * *

The SonaGate jolted to a stop. Giant scoop-doors clanged open. The bus was emptied quickly, as practiced, equipment and all. PreCorders had been situated by the technicians, and now record the smooth, orderly dispensation of the Maurian pageantry.

This—contrasted with the raggedy procession the Vuervee were sure to project—would certainly give all of Mauria a proud snicker.

Great platforms and seats were spread around for dignitaria and MarPrexMen. Colorful posters of Maurian events and traditions hung from trees around the meadow. Small pieces of wood and loose ground were vacuumed, and the tundra smoothed over.

The alloy of CO_2 Tubes glistened from all about. The big touch was the secret meeting table. Mr. Sir Councillor Blench fired a salutory SonaGun, and fourteen colorfully pageanted MarSekMen carried (with the hidden help of a mobile SonaLift) the gleaming alloy counter, joined on each side by two jewelled recliners. The pre-meeting festivities had begun.

Blench announced that Family Industries had donated the Pageantry for this meeting. The final pre-ceremony event, as CityMauria watched from home Corders, was a performance by the revered Cordioptric group, who enacted a grand scene.

The offering was a word-for-word, expression-by-expression reenactment of Mr. Sir Councillor Blench's climb to power. He blushed appreciatively, and applause was loud.

One MarPrex reporter was moved to button into his Corder: "I would find it hard to believe that the real event could have been any different in actions and words than the fabulous Cordioptric Troupe presented it. A moving, fulfilling experience."

None but Blench and Dunt knew that 40 Vuervee would be shot as the ring of killer Vuervee—not even the MarSek force that surrounded the meadow had a clue.

No, Dunt himself would operate the huge SonaGun.

The Vuervee that didn't die, would run.

All Mauria would see their Integrity returned.

All Mauria would see the "killer Vuervee" die impotently in the mud—the others fleeing.

All Mauria would see their High Hero, Mr. Sir Councillor Blench, stand over the dead bodies, his reign reborn.

Blench smiled tautly. Only one mark on his mood pulled at the heels of his mind. For now that this secret plan with Dunt was almost ripe, it somehow didn't seem as certain.

It was just that, somehow, out here in the wilds, so far from his element, a vague uneasiness clouded his mood.

Oh, Grell, it'll work fine. CounterFlow . . . CounterFlow . . .

* * * * * * * * * * * * * * *

Knives . . . Yes, knives. Now it's time again, so let's inhale a thousand knives. A rest now . . . why bother? We'll just stop, then the knives will go away. Don't get tricked . . . hold them in . . . can't . . . got to breathe. Eyes slitting open . . . first hot white light . . . blink . . . now weird colors . . . purple . . . green . . . hot orange-red . . . Oh, the knives . . . not quite so bad . . . but bad . . . scream . . . better now . . . cold . . . cold air . . . cold . . . eyes focusing now.

I'm dead. I remember . . . I died. Here on this rock . . . ran out of C02, I did . . . like a Grellhead . . . Oh, the knives again . . . ohh, these knives . . . must be alive . . . alive?

Young Trebel sat up. Her joints were stiff. She looked around. Hmmm. About 500Time, I'd say. Yes, 500. It's middle day, Ladies and Heroes, and here is young Trebel out in the hills, breathing Oxygen. Ha ha ho ho. Breathing Oxygen. He ha ha. No tube, he ho.

I must have died, she thought.

* * * * * * * * * * * * * * *

"Mark these words, Maurians! The Vuervee will pay for this insult to our culture! The Integrity of Mauria continues! These animals stayed away from our meeting because . . . they were afraid! Scared to death of . . . "

Mr. Sir Councillor Blench had been screaming into a Mauria-wide Corder for 20Time now. His mouth was purpled and twitching, jewels shaking SilverForm Wig askew. A hold-pin stuck out from his real hair.

A MarPrex Director was madly pointing to the approximate spot on his own head, waving his hand, trying to make Blench fix his wig. But this only made Mr. Blench more angry and he blurted louder.

" . . . to the Legal Council. What about my head, you rut! . . . Forget it. The people of the great Maurian empire . . . "

Mr. Sir Fruke shook his head. Too painful to watch, he thought. Fruke tapped the CorderMan gently, gave the "cut" sign.

Still bubbling and ranting, Blench noticed the pain-faced Mr. Sir Fruke, who had now walked directly between Blench and the Corder lens.

"You fool! You're in the view. If this is a cheap scheme by you and . . . "

"Mr. Sir Councillor Blench. The Corder has stopped. We're packing up. Get in the SonaGate." Fruke was speaking to a child. "Tomorrow we'll discuss strategy."

Blench started to bellow an angry retort, but all that escaped was a muffled breath. Mouth still frozen open, Blench bowed his head, licked his lips, and walked off to the SonaGate.

Across the meadow, the last engineer rolled up the last wire, scraped the disgusting wood-decay from its anti-static coating, thought about what a lousy job this was, kicked a fallen tree trunk and sprinted to the waiting bus.

He would be glad to get home.

The Maurians clanked away, and faded from the meadow, which was still covered with litter and pageantry.

And now, there was silence.

CHAPTER FIFTEEN
'Last Song of Spring'

Now, there were no knives. Hunger, yes, but no knives. And even hunger faded to unimportance for Trebel.

The air she breathed felt like a thousand flowers, now, instead of knives. Why was she alive? Could all Maurians adjust as she had? A barrage of questions came and went, and their sheer multitude drove her to more immediate thoughts. She must go to her cave, collecting plants on the way, and then sleep, Trebel thought.

Beautiful, untormented sleep replaced all goals. This miracle was yet too intense for her bruised mind.

Later to think.

* * * * * * * * * * * * * *

The Veem of Tedrin had undone its wombs, slung newborn young on vines, and had marched all day and into the night. They moved toward the tall peaks, still packed in snow. Hiola was especially happy, for life was moving to his snow peaks, away from Mauria, his destiny. His chunky form bounced with each step.

They had set off for a new valley to the West. The Maurians would be enraged, and better not to await their reaction.

But of Venes, his willowy legs stepped slowly, unhappily. He felt ignored, empty, and—angry. These fools! Now the Maurians were further than ever from speaking, from sharing secrets. And Venes was sure, the Vuervee were further and further from happiness. Well, *his* Veem would not live lives of the hunted. No. Here they were in the middle dark of night, and their souls fled instead of slept! Some forgot about survival! A voice interrupted his thoughts.

"So. My troubled brother sulks through the night." Hiola smiled down at Venes' rigid features. Hiolas' stocky form had caught up to Venes.

"I say, Hiola, were this Veem of mine, we would walk in the other direction . . . *towards* the Maurians, to end this running . . . "

"If you were Va, Venes, the Veem would not be of yours; . . . you would be of the Veem's."

"Why must everyone speak in Cir . . . ," this slipped Venes lips before he could stop.

A triumphant smile spread across Hiola's features. "I feel for you, Venes, your . . . "

"You'll watch, Hiola! Save your pity! I am right for this Veem, not you or Dillon, and I will prove it! If there is . . . "

"The *Circle* will prove what it . . . "

"Never mind this! I weary of this high talk, and then crawling away like the fools we are acting like. Crawling away like we have no place here! If there is no Vuerve who sees this . . . " Venes bottom lip jutted at the aloof Hiola, "I will *make* them see it! And then I will be their Va! And then all will listen to see what I hear the . . . the Circle tell me."

"But Venes, the Maurians *need* us, for *their* bloated bellies," Hiola argued, "we have no need of them. They . . . "

"They *can* be our friends, once they see us not crawl from life, they can help us with their . . . secrets, their knowledge of . . . "

"They are friends like the WhiteWeb is to the Needletree as it strangles its soil and days! Friends as the water is to the rock in the stream as it wears it to nothing!"

"You . . . just . . . want to be . . . Va," Venes accused.

"I can't control it if . . . " Hiola began.

"Why?! Why can't anybody *control* anything! Well, ... I can! I can control my life! And others! And I will prove this! Finally, and to all. And you can crawl all you want, all of you! I will *do* something about our dark lives of hiding! You will see!"

Venes stalked away from Hiola.

Hiola considered. He was disgusted by some of Venes words, but . . . the Circle has obviously chosen *him*, Hiola, to take the Veem as Tedrin approaches End. It must be, for lately Hiola pictures all Vuervee turning to him for guidance. This feels good! Proud Hiola, VeemVa Hiola! Who none ever listened to! Dillon has killed another! He can't be of the Circle. But . . . *all* are of the Circle, so how is this? The Circle chooses only those who are worthy! I am worthy! I am Hiola! I will be VeemVa!

The moon poked out from behind a cloud, and the Veem of Tedrin climbed a Whitebark-dotted ridge.

But as they reached the crest, and descended wearily into the next valley, and then up and down again, there was a Vuerve who had dropped back. Unseen. It was Venes.

As the Veem of Tedrin climbed ahead and down, then up a broad ridge, none saw that Venes was a vanishing mark, moving away . . . further and further toward the Plains.

And, much later, Venes reached the last EdgeHill, and gazed down upon CityMauria. The lights! The deep reds and greens and blues of the city—they were like his own colorhair! The shiny walls, the steam.

Venes walked again, stepping not from a hunters' path which aimed to the West Wall of CityMauria. *They* will listen, he thought, even as his own kind would not. And then they would all see, and would ask him to be VeemVa past Tedrin; and all would be well in the Veem of Venes!

* * * * * * * * * * * * *

Madness was upon the land, thought MarSekMan Meist. Now the Vuervee come to *Mauria* to be hunted! He checked the screens in his outpost along the West Wall. Yes, this multi-colored Vuerve trying to climb over the wall *into* Mauria—was alone. Hmmm. Made no sense. But what *had* lately?

He watched in humorous disbelief as Venes leaped upon the alloy, tried to climb up, then slipped to the ground, time and again.

Well, better call it into MarSek Command. Maybe they'll want to send this Vuerve to the lab.

He yawned.

Great shift they gave him, middle of the night.

His cooker beeped and a green light flashed. Ahhh, dinner, or early meal, . . . or whatever it was when you ate at *this* hour! His stomach turned with distaste as he remembered the tiny patty of oily Grell he had cooked. And suddenly, the Vuerve at the wall took on a different meaning.

After all, he had three more days and nights of this tedium. Several meals of Prime Vuerve would hardly make them more unpleasant! No, indeed. As a young MarSek patrolman, he hadn't eaten Prime in . . .

Meist chuckled, grabbed his SonaGun and opened the small portal at the base of the wall.

Venes walked slowly in, looking around, blinking at the steam and the lights.

He smiled broadly and held his hands up in a friendly gesture, though he could not see any Maurians.

"Maurians!" yelled Venes. "I have come for the meeting! I will speak to . . . "

Of certain, you will, laughed MarSekMan Meist.

The multiple beeps of the SonaGun could not be heard above the whooshing of the perimeter SonaVents.

Venes looked down curiously at his chest, started to protest, but fell dead before a word could be formed.

The many bright colors of Venes were hushed by the gray dust in which he now laid, unmoving.

And to the East, the Plains were turning red with dawn.

* * * * * * * * * * * * * * * *

Young Trebel was rushing down a torrid stream. She was surprised to find the boulders made of pillows. Each time a jagged rock met her flailing body, she tensed, only to find the rock a cushion from which to bounce playfully along.

And now a waterfall . . . its edge gaping over an unending pit. As she crested the stratified edge, she glimpsed an entire village below. Far, far below. The people of the village were building and playing. Brightly colored foilage grew into a ring of beauty.

Within, odd shaped dwellings sprung, made of the same lush growth. A smile glowed from every lip, and many young were playing. She saw from afar and near at once.

As she drifted closer, spinning ever so slowly in limbo, a change occurred in the village. Suddenly everyone was leaving. Just leaving. Wait! Wait for me! But it was taking too long for her to float down. Soon all the villagers had left, save one.

He was a brightly colored male, almost half Vuerven in appearance, and—yes—it was the face of the brave Vuerve whom she had watched the Maurian's encircle. He looked up at her, still too far away for words, and smiled bemusedly. Then he, too, had left.

Trebel leapt upright, awake. New day had dawned, and a bright blue sky yawned at her from the mouth of the cave.

She must leave! Why? What's happened to me? Now the memories flashed to her senses.

She was breathing Oxygen! Wild air! The shock caused everything to spin again, and she sat quickly to consider.

She perused her limbs. They seemed to reflect a different tone.

Not so white, a little Sun burnt; but most of all they radiated an unfamiliar color . . . an almost animal-like hue of tan.

She gathered her belt and tattered tunic. She looked at her spear, then snapped it off close to the point, inserting the now shortened reed into the remnants of her tunic.

She stepped from the cave into the glorious new day. She felt the air, she smelled the flowers. She heard the playful rustle of needle in breeze.

She giggled.

Her next step was . . . the Vuervee! She breathed their air, ate their plants. She would watch them from afar, and learn more of the tricks of enjoying this wild, wonderful wilderness!

She giggled again, and set off, away from the rising Sun.

Ho-de-hi! Off to more book adventure, everso!

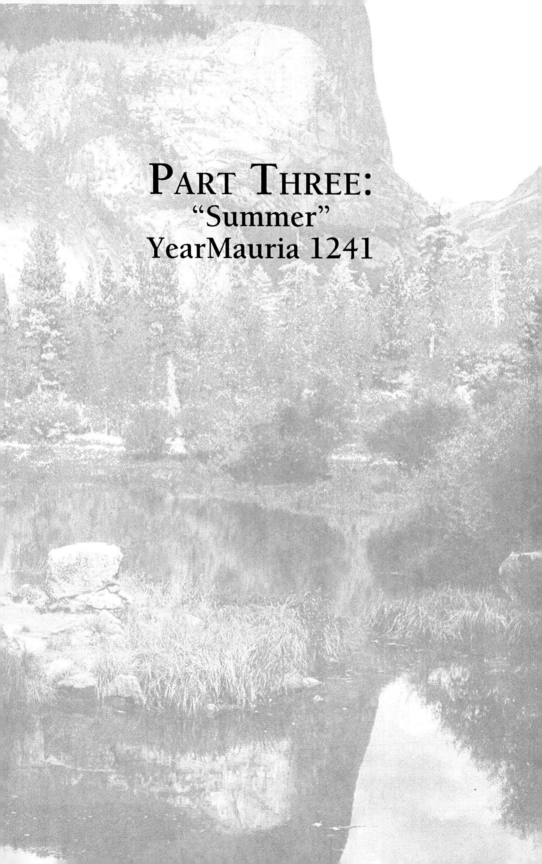

PART THREE:
"Summer"
YearMauria 1241

Chapter Sixteen
'Bordt'

The grainy alloy of the Legal Council building rose higher than all others in Mauria, and while some structures of half its height contained two and three levels, this justice hall had but one gaping interior: one cavernous, echo riddled hall, whose red ceiling arched massively above the metal squares of the floor.

The interior was a swirling array of reflections, an orange glow purveyed from the ceiling color. It was here that suggested crimes were agreed or denied. Crime in Mauria was rather sparse. It amounted to only six suggestions per day.

Of course, numerous crimes occurred between commoners. These were not tried, but were decided and punished on the spot by investigating MarSekMen.

Outside, CityMauria sweltered in middle Summer heat. Mauria's alloy FareWays and buildings could not be touched with bare skin. Most of Mauria wore alloy summer gloves for opening portals and the like.

Today, Mr. Sir Engineer Rute resided over the Legal Council. In Mauria, it was everyone's unilateral right to be judged by his betters. Rute's stern mouth and analytical glare commanded the hall from a six UniMeter-high podium. His metal voice charomed about.

" . . . hereto. This 189th day of YearMauria 1241. It is herefrom suggested that the Mr. Keest did present unaccounted for BookCredits to Family Industries' franchise #67-a-s, known as Terb's Independent Contracting Parlor."

"How do you explain, Mr. Keest?"

Mr. Keest pushed the "ARGUE" lever on the explanation stand far, far below. All Rute could see was the top of a black wisp of hair.

"Mr. Sir Engineer Resident Rute. I plead for denial. No sources can be breached. The BookCredits were obtained in the Integritorial search for advancement."

Rute ruffled the records, pronounced his decision. "This residium is in agreement with the suggestion. Fine is 300Book. Mr. Keest, the residium is not interested in considering the various exhausts and waste-products of Black Materials. If you can't advance in Mauria without leaving a trail, the residium will be forced to impose a ceiling on any further promotions. If nothing else, this will stop your sloppy gaming. Next, please."

There weren't any really challenging suggestions coming up, and Mr. Sir Rute considered instead his own affairs, which were in higher than high order, and he smiled the smile of the successor to the SilverForm Wig.

The folly of the Vuerven meeting had been most responsible for Rute's final push, Blench's final gasp. It was idiomatic in Mauria that one didn't fool with life-lines. Like food. Blench had, and lost.

Most of Mauria had witnessed the insulting event in the meeting meadow. This was a blinking SonaSign that Blench has lost control over the Vuerven food supply.

Blench was through. The Fruke-Rute coalition was on its way in. In a matter of days, Blench would find an advisory position offered to him on the Control Council; standard Grell.

His pride swelled. He would lead a race of Heroes, people who flourished in a mutated world where all but plant and Maurian had vanished. Well, the Vuervee survived too, but only as food.

While Legalites hustled about below, readying the next case, Rute pulled a small picture from his pocket. It was of Mr. Granes. The cliff of Granes' receding forehead wrinkled unsuspectingly from the image.

I will not peak the crest of power with that parasite on my neck! Then conjured, it will be interesting to see the actual flesh of the man who owned part of him. He will stare at Granes for a while, and then . . . Rute fondled the small SonaGun hidden beneath his tunic. And then . . . no more Granes! Ho-de-hi.

It won't be small gaming, he thought. It will be SilverForm Heroism!

* * * * * * * * * * * * * * *

Bordt sweated in the rippling heat above InterFare 67 N, checking his antique time-piece. He had a fat amount of time before his appointment at Family Industries' Hall of Records, so he looked for the cool of a RecParlor.

Some changes were noticeable about Bordt, including a new hairpiece and a tunic not seen often on a commoner. When he spotted Fleet's RecParlor, he grinned, displaying straight, white teeth—speaking of changes—and moved quickly to it.

Bordt's walk was more of a stalk, actually, for his posture bowed forward and his gait was mostly controlled by the toes. He almost looked like someone sneaking, but it was merely his displaced vertebrae.

In the portal, he clanged his tunic gratefully on the wall, wiped the sweat from his neck and smelled upon himself the un-mistakeable odor of sweat on metal—an intolerable aspect of hot days in Mauria.

But whatso! Sitting on a stool, half-soused as usual was his old friend, Mauv. She was a CommonerFemale of pre-historic roots, and happened to have the same missing tooth as Bordt—well, as Bordt *used to.*

He came upon her wire-haired, grumpy face, and declared, "I'll lay 50Book those grizzly claws of yours hold a Coyotia SourDrink with a smatch of Prickly Plum!"

"Bordt! You old robber, and how does . . . eh? Lookit this here! A shiny Mr. Sir's Forebar upon him . . . jest beneath his new hairpiece! And Grell if he don't have a new set of chewers! Don't you know a shine on the types o' you just makes the rust look worse?!"

"I'm still not too good for you, you old Parlor bum!"

"Hey," Mauv snided, "ye got somethin' goin' fer ya? Onto a big gamer, are ya?"

"You might say."

Bordt took in the sights of the room. The reception parlor was partially full. Those within it's red and gray striped walls were residue of a long morning's drink. They were ones whose lives had bogged and hardened, whether at the high, low or middle. There they would stay content, but everso the last to leave the parlors.

A pair of voices raised near a back booth. It was, thought Bordt, the unmistakeable prelude to a RecParlor brawl. Facting the facts, where FruitSour was served, Maurians would lose their CounterFlow. Bordt used to like the brawls, but they had tired from repetition.

It was always the same losers picking on the same, well-armed Mr.s. Why did a FruitSour make a Maurian think he could burst his Extract?

Bordt sipped his Coyotia Sour, the ferment fuming down his gullet. He and Mauv turned their attention to the two yelling in the rear.

"It wasn't that at all," the large one was saying. He had a large, less than prestigious mole on his nose.

"Says you," the chunky one said. His voice was calm and even. CounterFlow. "I'm not assertin' that you was wrong, . . . just coulda' been righter."

The larger one lost his calm. He was plainly saturated with much SourDrink.

Bordt grinned a tacky sneer, leaned to Mauv: "I go ye' 40Book on the smaller one over there. He's acting more Sour than he is, I'll say."

And now the tall one's immensity peeled from the counter, his jowls acquiver, and said, "Alben, you rejected Extract, step to the middle of this SourGrelled Parlor and defend your miserable Girl self."

The two faced off Parlor-center.

"You're *awl*ways right. And I'm *awl*ways wrong," Lins shouted at the smaller Alben.

"There, Lins, you see? We agree."

Applause rang loud among the observors.

Bordt chopped Mauv in the rib, winked a told-you grin. Alben mentally pounded Lins for another 10Time or so.

Bordt and Mauv turned away from the one-sided Integrity match.

"You tryin' to break yer Extract, Bordt?"

"Just Gamin' up higher, Mauv."

"You look silly and stupid all Hero'd up like that. Whatever yer game is, ye'll be back, Bordt. Then I'll like ye' again."

Over in the center of the room, Lins had smashed his SourDrink on the floor and headed for the portal in frustration.

Wasn't a very bloody brawl, reflected Bordt, as he watched Lins disappear onto the stream swirling above the FareWay. Another Maurian learns his place, avowed Bordt.

"Pay me next time, Mauv," Bordt said with a tinge of melancholy, "I know yer Book is thin."

Bordt concentrated on the gaming he had begun between Granes and Rute. Hmmm. Maybe one *couldn't* break one's mold. Everso, he would try. Like every Maurian, Bordt felt the rules didn't apply to him.

He exited the RecParlor, catching a crowded public SonaRail to the Family Industries Hall of Records, where he greeted his young ally behind a massive partition of shelves.

"I am most grateful," Bordt forced a wide grin.

"It's no medal off *my* tunic," shrugged Mr. Lope. "I took care of it straight away. Two days ago."

Bordt handed the Family Industries' clerk 1,OOOBook, winked at him, and left, leaving Recorder Lope awash in happy disbelief. The pay of 30Day in but a moment! Just to destroy the slim file which read, *"FAM IND, INDEP. CONTRS, GM PRLR: BORDT'S EXOTIC GAMING ROOM, 141N-22W."*

Whatso?!!

* * * * * * * * * * * *

Bordt arrived back at his GamingParlor just in time to see Mr. Granes shuffle near the walk. Granes followed Bordt into the gaming room.

The "Closed to Gaming" sign remained hoisted, and the pair walked into the back room. Bordt's stance and manner of hunched shuffle added to the mustiness of the ancient Parlor.

"Now then, Mr. Granes, *Sir*. You understand that this is a controlled business session with your buyer. As soon as he is convinced of the authenticity of your Black Material UniCopies, the deal will be set in motion."

Mr. Granes had been sucking noisily on a dry chew. He felt awkward, and just a bit common, in Bordt's back room.

"I hope, Bordt, that you realize why I can't let *you* show Rute the materials. Not that I don't . . . "

"Come, come Mr., one doesn't load a gun for another, now does one? As one who trusts no one ever, I admire your enlargin' skill at me own game."

Mr. Granes winced every time Bordt slipped into common talk, but his pride swelled a little anyway. After all, where small gaming was concerned, Bordt was the expert.

"But," realized Granes, "why have you piled all your machines and goods back here?"

Bordt didn't miss a beat.

"We want Rute to think he's gaming with losers . . . A Parlor that is losing Book. Eh? Now get your mask on."

* * * * * * * * * * * * * *

Mr. Engineer Rute programmed the EnvirCo SonaRail to deposit him a short walk from the small gaming room of Bordt.

He stepped onto the FareWay. During such hot weather, the steam hung in thick piles on Mauria. He sweated along with the dripping Fareway.

A large weather tunic of past days masked his executive clothing beneath. He was glad for the heavy fog. He didn't particularly care to be recognized.

The portal slid open for his entry. A slight mustiness gathered in the GamingParlor.

No one could be seen in the dim interior, but his footsteps signaled a creaky portal opening from the rear. He noticed a sign, on a bare wall. It read, "You are on your own."

Odd, he chuckled, most gaming Parlors were heaped with a myriad of gadgets and machines. Dust settled on bare counters here. And he knew why, thanks to his searching the FI Hall of Records last night!

The Mr. who appeared in the rear portal carried with him an alloy case, which dangled on a chain from his wrist.

"Sit down please, Mr. Engineer Sir Rute. I am Bordt. My small room is honored by your presence."

Ah, thought Rute. This is the fool himself! Granes! Because there *is* no Bordt. He had verified that at the Hall of Records. A poor ruse.

Oh, Granes had fixed a mask to his face, but he should have known that Rute would listen to Cordings of Granes' voice! There could be no mistake. The voice was that of second-rate exploiter Granes! This made it very simple, indeed.

Rute commended himself for such thorough preparation.

"As you can see, Mr. Sir Rute, the UniCopies are fused to my arm. Just a precaution. And the Corders are sealed in the next room.

They will record all that transpires, in the event you are moved by ambitious notions."

Me? Not Me!!

Rute found it hard to bury a smirk. The poorly camouflaged vent Corder was capped. Not only was there no Corder going, but even if there was, he could always blast his way into the back and destroy it afterwards.

He must admit, though, Granes deserved credit for ample imagination. If he hadn't already checked, he might actually believe there was such a place as Bordt's Exotic Gaming Room.

This was easy. Nothing like he had imagined. Perhaps Granes himself had become desperate, forcing a sloppy try at exploiting his materials?

But no, . . . it was just Granes being Granes, Rute smirked.

"May I see the Materials now, Mr. . . . Bordt?"

The words had floated for a moment in the dour air, and then both realized the blunder. In no situation would a Control CouncilMan refer to a SmallGamer as Mr., . . . unless . . . .

Rute reached for his SonaGun, as Granes struggled back to the portal, eyes gaping with terror.

But Rute was having trouble extracting the gun from his sitting position. He fumbled for it desperately. He had planned on being upright!

Rute cursed as Granes reached the portal and pressed the opener. He would get away!

Rute, in a frenzy, leapt to his feet, and was surprised to see the portal not opening for Granes. As he breathlessly pried the gun loose and fired, he heard Granes screaming, "No, no open it. Curse you Bor . . ."

The darts had patterned into his spine, near the lower back. Granes noticed all feeling leaving his body, then life flowed from his panicked form, and he turned to face Mr. Sir Engineer Rute.

A strange grin emerged through the pain as he slid down to the floor. He couldn't speak, but took last comfort from the now smug

Rute, who would also learn the finer points of small gaming rooms. The hard way, as Granes had.

Mr. Sir Engineer Rute couldn't quite fathom the odd grin on Granes' death-staring features. He hummed a little as he stepped to the corpse of his problem. The relief he expected to feel hadn't settled on him yet, but soon. . . . It was this disgusting room.

He took a metal box from his tunic, placing the unused darts and gun within. Then he connected the leads and watched the whole package incinerate in a puff, splaying a fine powder on the floor.

Next he withdrew a jewelry drum, set it to "DsCt," and positioned its braces and slides on the chain from Granes' wrist.

He squeezed the revolving joint, and with no more than a momentary "squish," had severed the alloy case of Black Materials from Granes' body.

Now a larger incineration case was assembled for the materials. He tried not to look at the pool of blood that drained from Granes' wounds as he ruffled through the UniCopies to make sure they were the real thing . . . yes.

At the top it said, "UniCopies, test here." He flipped his Corder to "VFY" and slid the mode to "UnCp."

A green glow from the indicator brought another grunt of satisfaction to Mr. Rute's nodding features. These were authentic, unreproduced Materials. At last . . . the final blemish . . . gone.

He thought of his face, the SilverForm-to-be face, now engaging in untold indiscretion. He knew of its parody. He prepared the Materials for incineration.

"Now, if you'll just step back from your little escapade, Mr. Hero, I won't kill you."

The first word had frozen Rute's expression in a crazy half smile of prior amusement.

His frame slumped back to the floor, eyes madly darting about the body, blood and paraphernalia surrounding him. Thinking was out of the question.

Bordt stepped out of the camouflaged side portal. "Whatso. Ho-de-hi. Mr. Sir, ye—I mean, you—have certainly made a mess of my establishment. Hmmmmn! Mr. Granes looks so much the worse with a full load of darts, don't you think? Oh, and listen. Please don't go into shock. This isn't the end of you at all. No, no. Your future is just about the same as when you first walked in here. Indeed.

"With one minor change, of course. But we have *time* to talk. You haven't really lost anything, just acquired a partner with a more powerful hold. Why, I'd say that between the Cordings of your nasty little actions today, plus Granes' materials, there's no need for worry, do you think? I mean, the package is unpriceable! Whatso!"

Mr. Sir Rute, who had regained a measure of alertness from Bordt's sarcastic reassurances, could not decide which was more grotesque: The hideous hole at the mouth of Bordt's gun or his slimy grin.

As his victim clutched for mental balance, Bordt pulsed with sensual anticipation. This was his very first high Hero of Mauria—brought to helpless surrender!

Bordt focused his tittilation on Rute's eyes. The eyes. The sudden vulnerability. The drop from smug confidence to weak, Girl-like subjugation! The esteem, the HeroShip, the control, it peeled away revealing the under-belly! Bordt shook with pleasure, felt it deep in his loins, and a gasp of release bubbled from his mouth. Bordt's eyes widened as a wave of pleasure threatened to crest over him.

And then it was over, and Bordt blew a calming, settling breath.

And the shock was over for Mr. Sir Rute, also.

Rute sighed, coming back to reality—tarnished as it was—and ceremoniously regained his composure, stance and expression. This was life in Mauria. Everso.

"Ah, yes. Very good, Mr. Sir Rute. We need you looking like the great leader you are. Now don't we?"

Rute sighed, "I don't know. Do we?" Bordt smiled, "Oh, yes. Yes, we do."

CHAPTER SEVENTEEN
'Lola'

There was a circle of tall, ice-capped peaks. They stood silent form against the great whipping storms at their tips, where no life could grow. But below the great crags of snow, even below the broad Whitebark-coated bases of these mountains, a joyous mating to Summer was happening.

In the core of this great circle of white peaks was Lola, the valley of Lola, where even Maurian maps couldn't dream of such a lush plant-thick valley green, and red and blue and yellow and brown! All this was nestled deep within the folds of the cloud-piercing peaks.

It was here amidst a radiant ground carpet of Mindo's blue reed leaves, Coyotia's rich green stepped chutes, the bright yellow stripes of red Cuervos, and the deep friendly brown of Torna; that the Veem of Tedrin played and basked under middle Summer's sky of white-patched turquoise.

But of all the growths in Lola, none was loved more than the Redfruit trees of the lower valley. It was on these round, crunchy and juicy, white-filled apple fruits that the Veem would feast in early Autumn.

But now, the apple fruits hung from whorled branch, a greenish pink.

As gangly Grespuin looked about, he saw many Vuervee Menting to this lush valley of Lola. For such beauty and fertility to lie in the shadow of the barren snowpeaks on all sides, surely this spoke of a Sun behind all clouds, a fire in every snow. A beginning in every End.

Tiny Erdeurr stepped through the high arrow leaves nearby and he grinned easy greeting to Grespuin.

"The beauty here is such that few friends think of play," said Grespuin, atwinkle. "If, Erduerr, we chase and jump through Lola, others will see of the beauty of play in a beautiful place!"

"Yes," agreed Erduerr. "Their mouths of tense Menting will flower to smiles of fun."

An impish grin colored Grespuin's bony face, he arced his reedy form to the sky. He screamed: "EEEEEEEEEE, uughghgh, EEEEEH!"

Grespuin and Erduerr hopped to a flailing, giggling romp about the Veem. Many who Mated, many who Mented, many who lazed, were disturbed by the sudden crash of twig and form. Others grinned and leaped to join the run.

Soon, a broad wave of Vuerven color swept through Lola, and their many screams and laughs echoed to the brim of the snow peaks.

There were two Vuervee who were jostled by this romping tide and moved their aged bodies quickly behind a bush, to avoid being trampled. They smiled at the young energy, and some of the old! They were Tedrin and his sister, Colia, who had left her Veem far to the North for a visit.

Of she and Sereoul and Tedrin, Colia was the broadest of feature. Her yellow waisthair of past seasons had changed to white from the bitter cold of her home ground. Her sturdy limbs seemed ever to plant themselves against an icy wind. She was taller than Tedrin; shorter than their brother, Sereoul, whose Veem lived far South.

"I miss," said Colia, "the lightness here." She and Tedrin reverted back to the soft patch of grass on which they had been sunning.

"Would you reflect your form upon a pond, you would see the beauty your land of small Sun has carved into your soul, dear sister."

Colia's form was a melody of muscle, burning white in the Sun. Her cheeks showed the lines of many cold Changes.

"Yes, Tedrin, but this also speaks of hardness. There is little time for growth of the mind, Menting, studying the Circle. We study the tundra, for signs of food; we study the clouds for signs of snow."

"This sounds very hard."

"In many ways. We have a trouble called Seegrid by us. When a friend is too much alone, for too long; the barrenness enters the soul. For days a friend will moan and mope, sometimes to End."

"It is that barren?"

"Only to the eye, but often we are only of the eye. For beneath the frozen tundra is a thin but teeming world of life. Ice berries, Spangle plants and Keori struggle one upon the next for life. And we are proud of life there! That we stand to the cold, the small Sun. But of you, dear Tedrin?"

"I am old, Colia. Just very old. I know I will End soon. I have seen it in a vision. I have . . . been very happy in my setting Sun."

"I, also. How does the Veem of Sereoul do?"

"I know not, it has been a Spring and Winter since last we saw him."

"And of Venes, Hiola and Dillon; their Circles?"

"Hiola and Venes are a whole between them. If I could but make them a single being, they would grow with the Circle. Hiola clutches to the Circle as if it is something to drag around everywhere one goes. Venes shuns the Circle as if it wanted to spin him over a cliff.

"Dillon seems balanced of himself, but has been through many twists, everso. I have told Dillon of the Maurian and our Mother, Blisfur. He is out searching for Venes, who has been missed for long. I fear Venes has gone off alone, somewhere."

"Much has weighed on you to see the thorn and not the flower."

"You are, ever, as love, Colia."

"We wither together in the Sun. A pair of silly, dried fruits!" And they both laughed, and hugged; and felt the Sun on their faces.

* * * * * * * * * * * * *

In a dark forest of spiring Cuervo trees, Trebel's long, newly muscled legs flashed in the beams of light which shafted to the ground. As she streaked through the cone-littered ground carpet, Maurian darts ripped and teared after her; raising pocks of dirt, shredding bark from trees.

Ruts! Shooting at their own kind!

How many times must she streak for her life, anyso?!

They had come upon her around a curved canyon wall, the hunters had. For a moment, she had started to hail them, with a wave, forgetting how she must look to them. The hunters excited motions and the aiming of their SonaGuns reminded her quickly, and she bolted with her newly developed agility.

She plotted a course at a mound of snow peak, barely poking over the horizon to the West. If she could put enough distance between the MarSekMen and her before late day she could escape for good in the night forest. This far West from Mauria, she knew they would return to its walls before dark.

And so she ran, her tortured lungs screaming their protest. She knew that each rise, each stream, each stand of indifferent forest she traversed, might be the difference.

An icy spring numbed her legs as she waded through it, Torna clumps tore at the remnants of her tunic; and she weaved, tumbled and staggered on.

And soon a valley was passed, and then a grassy knoll, and then a high walled canyon, and still she pushed over and beyond her limits, into another valley, over another bluff, down along a stream bed.

And she had left the Maurians far behind. But far enough? She didn't know. It was early afternoon, they still had time.

And now, near a gentle knoll, young Trebel's thin knees buckled.

And now she crawled, gasping for breath, gasping for one more valley between her and the MarSekMen.

* * * * * * * * * * * * *

Hearing a clumsy snapping of twigs and ground cover, Dillon quickly climbed a tree, hiding high in the upper boughs. He had worked his path many ranges towards Mauria from Lola, seeking sign of Venes. This noise must mean the enraged Maurians have taken after the Veem of Tedrin. He poised for utter stillness as the noise approached.

But the battered soul which stumbled and wheezed into view hardly posed a threat. Trebel's tortured face moved beneath the tree he was in.

He saw a flash of . . . green?

A Vuerve?

No . . . it was the same silly Maurian girl who hid in a bush on the day the Maurians surrounded him in the meadow.

Was she, then, hiding from the Maurians?

She was quite thin, too, from lack of food, he guessed. He felt her pain, her struggle, and an odd desire moved his form. He would speak to this one, so determined.

As she passed beneath him, Dillon dropped upon her, snagging her hands with his, in case she tried to grab the reed stuck in her ragged tunic. His carefulness was of small need.

She could barely stand, even with his armlock supporting her. He spun her and saw Duerr's Birthgem around her neck.

A pulse of bright anger flashed within Dillon. Her neck writhed dangerously close to Dillon's infuriated arms. He shook her and thought of Duerr. And then he shook her again. And he would kill her, but for her weeping. She bent limply.

A Maurian crying?

He gently rested her in the damp ground carpet, bewilderment furrowing his eyes.

"Who are you?" asked Dillon.

"It . . . doesn't matter."

"You are Maurian, but use no tube."

"It . . . just happened. One day."

"You are of the Circle?"

"The what?"

"The Circle. You have color in your headhair."

"What are you going to do with me?"

"Are you running from the Maurians?"

"Yes."

"You are very thin."

"Yes."

"How do you have Duerr's Birthgem?"

"His . . . oh, this. I killed him."

"You . . . before, when I saw this friend of mine on your neck, I almost . . . "

"What?"

"Killed *you!*"

"Can this be? One of the great unkillers speaking so?"

"Yes," said Dillon, missing the sarcasm.

"I've never . . . spoken to a Vuerve; before your friend, and now you. You . . . frighten me. Speaking to a Vuerve is strange, wrong. I was used to *eating* you, not *talking* to you."

Dillon slapped young Trebel on her cheek, snapping her head back.

"You'll lie in pieces before another Vuerve nourishes you!"

"I . . . didn't mean . . . "

"We say what we mean. You must fend for yourself. I go."

He threw her to the ground, stomped away.

"In Mauria . . . ," this stopped Dillon's receding form, "In Mauria we don't always say what we mean."

Dillon kept his back to the sprawled Trebel for long, then asked, "But how can this be? To it, a tree bears apple fruits, not Coyotia. You *must* speak from yourself. What else can you speak from?"

"Would you . . . I mean," Trebel was choking on her words, "would you hide me? I haven't the strength to run anymore. They will kill me. Your friend, Duerr, he . . . showed me a new way for eating, so I wouldn't kill. He died with a smile. I . . . sensed to take his jewel. He smiled when he died. Please."

The last was spoken with such downtrodden dignity that Dillon considered, looked at her green streak, which now spread from ear to neck.

"You eat plants? Only?"

"Yes."

Dillon walked close to her. He bent upon his knees, and Mented to her; his forehair brushing her knee. Trebel still gasped for breath.

Finally his form straightened again.

"There is something within you. You are not what you seem. There is a part of you which . . . "

Trebel gazed into Dillon's eyes, clinging to buds of compassion which lay near the bottom of their deep blue pools, flanked by his rugged, smooth cheeks.

"I am Trebel," she said, a little impishly.

"I am Dillon. I will hide you. Follow me."

Dillon helped the exhausted Trebel to the base of a Whitebark, under which a large patch of clover grew. He carefully pried the wide carpet of gold and blue trumpets, guided her under it, and covered her, leaving a small slit for breathing.

Young Trebel could dimly see Dillon's shrinking silhouette as he left, and a pillow-warmth covered her tattered body.

She held very still.

Trebel didn't know how much time went by as she straddled exhaustion, fear and the waves of dreamy sleep.

There was a crunching of metal boot on ground cover which pounded closer and closer to Trebel's half-consciousness.

Soon, four MarSekMen stood not a tree's length from her covered womb.

She heard them curse and then head East for CityMauria, to beat the falling Sun.

Trebel plunged into a deeper, peaceful sleep. The Earth closed about her weary form, and was her warm, soft blanket.

CHAPTER EIGHTEEN
'Silver Rute'

" . . . Blench gracefully accepted the position of prestigious Advisor to the Heroic Control Council. Mr. Sir Blench officially removed the SilverForm Wig, inserted the Silver Key into the Sona sealed Portal and was visibly appreciative of his new advisory office. Mr. Sir Engineer Rute, acting head of Council, flanked by Mr. Advisor Bordt, expressed his . . . "

Dunt angrily snapped his Corder down. The Grell was *really* flying today. Yes, and someone else was riding it to glory. Well, he had picked losers before, but Blench turned out the biggest. So, another year for him. But those Girlhead politicans! Those Family Industries Grell eaters! Fruke and Rute. And that weird Bordt fellow. Some kind of advisor, who had come out of nowhere.

Mr. Sir Dunt practiced his Heroic grimace into the reflector. Then he spat on the floor.

After all, any Hero who would live with a girl—they called them Ladies! Soppering, weak house cleaners is what they were!

The day a MarSekMan becomes Councillor—the day *he* became Councillor—that would be the end for girls. At least in Mr. Sirs' homes. You can lay Book on that! No wonder Mauria was loose at the edges. How could anyone run a civilization with a girl in every Hero's room?!

At least Rute wasn't from FI—even if he *did* have a Lady. Mr. Sir Dunt had now worked to a boil. He couldn't sit.

He arranged his alloy Terrain pieces on the large military counter before him, but couldn't concentrate.

Corder bank "E" blinked its red eye open. Hmmm. Whatso? He flipped for communication contact.

"This is Dunt. I got a light on you, go ahead."

The crackle of a MarSekMan's voice temporarily lifted Dunt's seething boredom.

"Ho, this is group E, we're at . . . uh . . . coordinates 2-North, 198-West. MarSekMan Quate reporting. We had spotted one Vuerve, which we lost moving in a Westerly course . . . pretty true to . . . coordinate 2 North. It escaped past our safe-zone for night return. . . . We're headed back now. No signs of any Vuervee . . . uh . . . except that one. This is Quate, on return, x code 6, Sir."

"Code 6, Quate, you're on your way."

Drool! 200 MarSekMen and just one animal spotted! Dunt lit the transparent map on the wall. His eyes tracked West of Mauria, past the 198th Western Coordinate. He considered. Well, they can't be further West than that; there's nothing but barren snow peaks. No food, nothing. The drooling ruts have really pulled a fast one. They must be far North or South.

One thing's sure, someone better find them quick. The population of CityMauria hadn't been told about the food shortage; but they would figure it out soon enough . . . as more and more Grell found its way to their plates.

And what after that?

The herd up North wasn't yet big enough to trim, and the Southern Vuervee were too hard to catch; all that desert and those endless hills. A hunter's nightmare, to be sure.

Dunt's stomach screamed with tension, with unreleased frustration. His skin prickled with anger. He undressed, and lifted weights for a bit, trying to exhaust his irritation; then searched his nude form in reflection.

Grell! He was *proud* of his MarSek-thin body. What did they expect? A Hero can't last half a search mission with the blubber of civilians!

Used to be, Maurians *admired* streamlined forms. Like the Vuervee. Fantastic lines and strength, those animals. Their skin flinching and rippling its gamey tone.

Dunt rubbed hands over his muscle-squat thighs. The texture excited him.

Ah. None of this was helping. What a joke! The real Heroes were out hunting the hills for the Vuervee. He, the grand Hero of all, scanned dials and screens for coordinates and numbers.

A girl's lot if ever there was!

"Ebrag," he snapped into the Corder, "come in here!"

1stLevel Attache Ebrag leapt through the portal, shaking his head, hanging his just-awakened, sleep-loose face.

"Ebrag, did you finish classifying my game pieces?"

"Yes, Hero Dunt. I was just . . . "

"You were just sleeping. Whatso. No one has any energy lately. A MarSek designed Field Day is what we all need!"

"Yes, Hero."

Dunt looked thoughtfully to Ebrag's small face, his enormous deep black eyes.

"Ebrag . . . that . . . little commoner thing you found me last time?"

"I'm afraid she won't come again, Hero. You . . . permanently injured her, and . . . "

"Grell-grell-grell-grell-gurrellll! She must have fallen! Or hurt herself after she left here. You know I just talk to them, Ebrag! You know that?"

"Yes, Hero."

"Hummphg. Get her anyway. Or I'll shove her in the WorkHouse."

"She is there now, Hero."

"Augh . . . . Ebrag, what of that quarters cleaner? Is she still here?"

"Yes, Hero. But, . . . if I may, Sir, I have helped her to seek LadyShip. Her Extract is good, and . . . "

Ebrag's tenor waived gratingly on Dunt's restless frustration. "Whuuuu-aat! *My* attache! Girl-soft?!"

"It's really nothing, Mr. Sir. And her certification is two days from now, and if you—*change* her . . . she won't . . . that is . . . "

"Now you're calling me a Matist!?" Dunt's voice lowered to a threatening growl, "E-brag . . . bring her in! *Now*, if you like your uniform. *And*," he halted the Attache's exit, "you will *see* what girls are for. You will watch. You will see their weakness.

"Remain here," Dunt steamed on, "I will fetch her. We wouldn't want you sneaking your Corder in, now would we?"

Ebrag covered his resentment with CounterFlow until Dunt disappeared through the portals.

He awarded himself a quick smile and dialed on his Box.

"Yes?" a voice crackled in answer.

"Mr. Bordt, I haven't much time. If you can speed someone over here, I'll leave his back portal vulnerable."

"You're growing up, Mr. *Sir* Ebrag. Welcome to Mauria. Your BookCredits will be under your locker. Your female friend shall receive her LadyShip papers. I suggest you make yourself . . . unavailable for a few days. In case Dunt seeks personal retribution."

"Thank you, Mr. AdvisorSir."

* * * * * * * * * * * * * *

" . . . became a standing ovate when Mr. Sir Rute finally accepted the nomination. All through the streets, MarPrex unveiled giant posters of the new Engineer Hero. In his recognition speech, the new leader of the people reminded all Mauria of his reluctance at such high post, and asked for the help of all to re-establish the Integrity of Mauria and the plentiness of Vuerven food. Within moments, Mr. Sir Bard of MarSupply was heartily . . . "

"Ummm. Not bad, eh, Mr. Sir Councillor Rute?"

"Good enough, Bordt."

As Rute reclined spread-legged on the silver couch at lN-lW, Bordt's arched, humping body paced across a silver rug in the grandest room in Mauria; the office of the SilverForm Wig. Everything in the room, from chair to floor to books, emanated its silver shine.

"Quite a change from your roots, eh, Bordt? You have _my_ admiration, that's so. Hah! Advisor to the Councillor of all Mauria! From a small gamer! Hah. It's . . . beautiful. And you're calling the shots, to boot!"

"Not to detract from high politics, Mr. Sir, but after scrounging the survival of an independent GamingParlor; this high Hero stuff is just so much drool."

"I wouldn't underestimate the . . . "

"_You_ are the one who underestimated _me_, Rute."

"You've got a sting to you, Bordt, that's sure. Lucky for me you didn't go for the SilverForm Wig yourself! Hah, now _that_ would have been funny. From ParlorMan to Councillor of all Mauria!"

Bordt smiled, and thought; how quickly you forget _your_ roots, Mr. Sir Councillor. But Bordt said:

"There are _some_ things one can't do, no matter how clever. No, Mr. Sir Councillor, that is beyond my scope, I'm afraid. I'm content to be Advisor for a few years, Rute, and then, maybe, . . . who knows?"

"Well, Bordt, where do we go from here?" Rute asked, fingers kneading the SilverForm Wig atop his head.

"How would the new Councillor handle it?"

"Well, I would try to renegotiate a meeting with the Vuervee under the idea of a new Maurian leader, a new Maurian cooperative."

Bordt's squinty eyes considered patronizingly. These high Heroes were just fluff, he thought.

"Fair. Fair enough. But these are troubled times, Rute."

Mr. Sir Councillor Rute still flinched at the lack of pre-respected title.

"Maurians want their dignity back," continued Bordt. "Why be Grellin' around showin' yer *need* for talkin'? Ye' . . . ," Bordt took a breath. He had fallen into commoner talk. He started again. "Why exhibit a desire to negotiate? If we have control over the food supply, then let's show it."

"How?"

"Simple, Mr. Hero. We'll grab the most massive Vuerven catch in history. A *military* hunt that can't fail. For the next while, Grell will be a thing of the past. A Mauria of contented stomachs and BookCredits will greet you cycle next."

"But . . . that will deplete the herd!"

"Yes, but now we'll have Mauria behind us . . . their stomachs and their BookCredits will say so. *Then* we'll worry about a depleted herd."

"That's a big *then*! We're not gaming for Parlor items, here, Bordt. You're talking about our *food supply*!"

Bordt just stared at Rute. There was no respect in this glance. These high Mr. Sirs . . . they were afraid of their own boot vents!

"Dunt won't buy it, anyso," Rute tried. "The head of MarSek would never allow . . . "

"Dunt has no choice."

* * * * * * * * * * * * * * * * * *

As the day wore old in CityMauria, the nerve centers of the great metallic beast were leaping with activity, and much overBook was made. With hunting confined—so far, unsuccessfully—to the military, the biggest stress was on MarSupply.

Mr. Sir Bard, whose bulbous belly suggested he sampled all he distributed, was frenetically riding priorities to their limits. Which Integritorial dinner party would receive less Prime? What level of Mr. must Grell his way through the next 6period? Can a Mr. Sir be asked to add a small amount of Grell to his diet? Just for now?

And at LifeCo, hundreds of hunting quota personnel were shifted to the reproduction functions. Mr. Sir Burn was tearing his hair, because in the Hall of Futures reproduction center, a group of contractors were trading future *meat* for Extract! Legalities were investigated, new precedents ordained.

EnvirCo's engineering department was flailing with over-loaded relays as *everyone* was on public CompBoxes, deluging quota-predictions.

MarPrex was in a tizzy handling complaints, shuffling out news releases which tried to anticipate the *next* group of complaints. And Fruke drove the team on, pushing bleary-eyed scribers beyond themselves.

CityMauria was no longer stale and bored.

The Parlors were full, the walks were crowded, and Maurians were drawn close together by the basic drive common to them: challenge!

And on FareWay 34 N, a top security SonaRail sped Mr. Sir Councillor Rute and Mr. Advisor Bordt to Dunt's MarSek Command Center.

* * * * * * * * * * * * * * * *

Mr. Sir Dunt had been shocked at the hunched, clawed form of Mr. Advisor Bordt, as he trailed Rute through the portal. Bordt's expensive ForeBar of hand-formed silver, immaculate tunic and well styled hair had been unable to hide a certain commonness of demeanor. The tight, rigid stance; the darting nervous eyes; the absence of Integritorial aloofness. From whence, Dunt had thought, does *this* strange pair come?

Leave it to Rute, the first Councillor from Engineering, to trash up the high office with all kinds of raff. Even the SilverForm Wig looked appalled at its station atop Rute's features. Drool!

And now, SourDrinks in hand, Dunt capsulized the crisis to Rute and Bordt.

"Quite simple, really, a grit of a twist. We're unable to locate the local Vuervee anywhere. They could be North, South or could even have circled around us and struck across the plains for the sand beaches East of here. They could be anywhere from mountain to desert to ocean.

"The problem with the herd of Southern Vuervee is that the time and expense for hunting them appears too great for the immediacy of our little . . . bind.

"This leaves the Northern group. Easily found, anyso, but of too small a size to trim and still get a yield worth anything. Whatso?!"

"Then," piped Bordt, "Rute's plan is the only out."

"What plan is this," asked Dunt skeptically?

"Uh, yes," Councillor Rute stammered, groping," I meant to tell you this earlier, Dunt, but, um, Mr. Advisor Brodt has studied it more thoroughly—under my advisement, of course—and he can get into the technical details better."

Ah, thought Dunt, the steam clears. It is not Rute dragging this repulsive Bordt by the ears . . . it is Bordt, with his hand up Rute's tunic. Ho. It will never work, Dunt thought. Easy for me to alert Fruke to all this.

After all, it was supposed to be *Fruke's* Rute, not *Bordt's* Rute! Fruke, with Dunt at his side, will never stand for this! Hi-ho! I am back in the game.

"The plan is quite simple, really," Bordt spoke in his low grind," we will take the entire Northern herd all at once. This will provide Mauria with enough supply until your MarSekMen can locate the main herd locally."

"That's it?!" Dunt asked, eyes astounded.

"That's it," rumbled Bordt.

"You've flipped your Wig, Rute! If we do that, there'll be no reproduction from the North. Why, do you realize we have held back on that herd for six years; and, now, they're just starting to reproduce to trimmable size! And you're going to . . . "

"That is correct, Dunt," said Rute. "The plan entails . . . "

"Rute, Councillor or not, I'll see to it that . . . "

"Hold back," said Bordt, "Eh, perhaps Dunt has a point, Mr. Sir Councillor Rute. And look here," Bordt flashed a glance at his time piece, "you're already late for the MarPrex interview sessions, so, eh, why don't you Rail for 1N-1W, Sir, and Dunt and myself will discuss alternative plans; I'll fill you in later?"

"Well," said Dunt, "I *do* have some rather interesting thoughts about how we can . . . "

"Well, fine," said Rute, grateful to be out of it, "I'll . . . uh . . . speed on my way then. And with a nod of SilverForm Wig, Rute was gone, flanked by the waiting MarSekMen.

As their footsteps receded through the rear portals, Dunt confronted Bordt.

"Bordt," threatened Dunt, "now that we're alone, I'll tell you whatso. I don't know what your game is, but you're way over that slimy head of yours. The other members of the Council and I will . . . "

"Do nothing."

"All right, let's be intelligent . . . commoner. Show me your strength or get out of here. I'll put it that simple."

They locked eyes.

Dunt immediately knew there was something.

Under his tunic, in his loins, Bordt felt another strong surge of sensual excitement rise up. How would *this* high Hero fall from smug disdain to helpless, girl-like surrender? All the faces came back again. Those moments. The sudden washing away of all Integrity. The emergence of naked, vulnerable defeat. Slavery.

Bordt closed his eyes, savoring the coursing pleasure building up and up. He was having a FieldDay with all these high Heroes!

He unloaded.

"UniCopies of Mr. Sir Dunt, high Hero of MarSek, engaged in compromising behavior with a lovely young quarters-cleaning Girl."

Bordt watched Dunt's eyes, watched the superior and the Heroic peel away. Now he watched the first drops of fear, confusion, shock.

And as Dunt crumpled into the nearest chair, Mr. Advisor Bordt's face turned away to release a short gasp of emotion, of pleasure, of completion.

And, again, in Bordt's loins, it was over.

Bordt regained his composure and turned to Dunt.

Dunt clapped his hands together, staring into a great void which had settled in the space immediately in front of his eyes.

Finally, Dunt nodded, pursing his lips in wry appreciation, and just that fast, had adjusted. He had already put the loss behind him, and spoke to Bordt matter-of-course, as if they were always a coalition. A true Maurian.

"Fruke will have to be placated," Dunt said. "He has been expecting to move in after Rute. I will tell him this . . . mass hunt won't work—that Rute will hang himself with it. That will cover Fruke. I will then assemble my best MarSek unit for harvesting the entire Northern Vuervee herd. We will leave tomorrow. I will personally supervise the campaign.

"Mr. Bordt, give me all you want done now. I will not live with a parasite on my Integrity. Tell me what I have to do for those UniCopies. I will do only that, and no more."

Bordt was amused at Dunt's strength of acceptance, his practicality. "And if I don't return them to you? What will you do? You have no choice."

"I will kill you and myself."

Now it was Dunt's turn to lock Bordt's eyes.

Bordt saw immediately that this MarSekMan was not gaming. A thought struck him: *You can't game someone who's willing to lose it all.*

"I see," offered Bordt. "All right, I'm glad to deal straight ahead. This is refreshing. These are my terms: First, we'll promote this Northern herd as the ring of killer Vuervee, that way, they'll . . . "

"Serve a double function," Dunt finished. "Food for starving Mauria and a medal for Rute's new regime."

"Quite correct. Mr. Sir Councillor Rute will actually *accompany* this Heroic MarSek expedition as a publicity dart."

"So you can kill him, Bordt, and grab the Wig for yourself?"

"No, so *you* can kill him and grab the Wig for me."

In the hanging silence, Bordt and Dunt stared deep into each other's eyes once again.

Finally, Dunt nodded, a growing respect in his eyes for the ugly man before him.

"And then," he said, "I will have my UniCopies? And I will remain commander of MarSek?"

"Upon my ascension to the Silver Office. Those are my terms, and yours."

"So be it. Rute is dead. Died, fighting the killer Vuervee. Where . . . did you come from Bordt?"

"The gaming district."

"I should have known. The gaming district. Well done. Commoner to Councillor in four easy LogiSteps."

"Mauria, Mr. Sir Dunt, is just one large gaming parlor. Mr. Sirs are far easier to game than most of my ex-customers. It's just . . . no one ever thought to burst their Extract before me. Mr. Sirs are too concerned with Integrity to do what it really takes."

"So you want the power, eh?"

"All the way. But not for itself, anyso. I will retire very quickly, for the wealth and leisure. I am, after all is said, a gamer; I look for profit and challenge, not Heroism. Heroism and Integrity can't buy a thing. Beating high Mr. Sirs is not enough of a challenge."

"Rute must be killed by bare hands, Dunt, so the Vuervee are blamed."

"Everso, Mr. Bordt."

* * * * * * * * * * * * * *

Of any ten gameboards sold by Family Industries' amusement and recreation section, seven were Terrain boards. The game of Terrain was the soul of the Maurians.

Ironically, the game itself was invented by a low-ranking Mr. of MarSupply, Mr. Treunt. As if to reaffirm the *real* rules of Mauria, though, a section Councillor named Mr. Sir Bunt usurped credit for Terrain's conception. It was not until his death declaration was opened that he proudly advised of the real inventor (who was also dead by then).

It was also generally agreed that the usurper showed more Heroism than the inventor, because he *recognized* the game's potential. The thinking was that Mr. Treunt, the inventor, illustrated inferior skill at his own game when he carelessly let its rewards slip from grasp.

Now, in the SilverForm lounge, Mr. Sir Councillor Rute and Mr. Advisor Bordt had decided on a round of Terrain to unwind from a tricky session with MarPrex reporters.

Much searching had ensued, revealing that the giant, silver Terrain game in residence at lN-lW had been taken away for cleaning. More investigating led the pair to a servant's room where a Commoner's board and pieces were annexed by Rute.

And so they had settled in for a relaxing evening of mental combat, drinking, and munching on dried Prime chips served by the lN-lW staff.

Bordt now squinted happily over the board. He would win, he thought. Rute squirmed and coughed a little, searching for a comeback strategy. Rute rubbed his eyes, and attacked a piece of Bordt's.

Bordt calmly lifted the surrounded, isolated piece from the board, displaying the large black "T" under its base. This was the Terrain piece—and anyone unknowingly attacking it would most surely lose the game. He moved it to homesquare and the game seemed over.

But the thick lips of Rute were chuckling. His eyes were ecstatic.

"Look, Bordt! You're missing a piece. No one wins! You can't complete the Array."

"What?! But Grell! It's not . . .*fair*! Drool! Some trashy commoner loses a piece to his set and . . . "

Rute enjoyed Bordt's helplessness.

Bordt slammed his fist on the counter, rattling the room. His skin turned red, his lips bubbled. Bordt could not stand unforeseen events! It was one of the few times anyone had seen the veteran ParlorMan without CounterFlow.

Rute smirked, soaking it in.

"There's no such thing as that!!" Bordt screamed. He paced about the room, kicking recliners, shouting.

Then he noticed Rute's wry smile.

Bordt smiled, too, and went to the counter cabinet to refill SourDrinks for both of them.

Rute shook his head in appreciation, leaned back with the drink Bordt handed him.

"What are *you* so rattled about, Bordt? *I'm* the one that has to leave for the wilds tomorrow!"

The drinks were beginning to make Rute feel quite on top of the world. The intoxicating activities of the new Councillor of Mauria plus the fruit ferment were lighting his complexion with rolling bravado.

"Tell me about the packages, again, Bordt. Tell me. It'll make the long ride in the SonaGate more bearable."

"Well, Sir, when your expedition locates the Vuervee up North, the MarSek Corders will have a picture of you, SilverForm Wig in the foreground, 'killer' Vuervee in the background. Then, when the Heroic mission returns with Prime Vuervee for every table in Mauria, that picture will be on the package. The Councillor who wasn't afraid to go in the field and *personally* secure the Maurian food supply!"

"What a touch, Bordt! You are absolutely *mad* with cleverness!

Councillors will turn to the gaming parlors for advisors from here in. Hi-ho! And to think I was *worried* when you caught me with Granes! It was the luckiest day of my life."

Bordt smiled a modest acceptance of this praise.

CHAPTER NINETEEN
'Cloud Pole'

The valley called Lola by the Vuervee had seen much gentle summer peace and fun for Tedrin's Veem. Beneath bubbly, billowy clouds which puffed in a light blue sky; Yenda plant was snacked on, Mindo seeds were cooked, splashes were taken in warming streams and much learning and reflection was done. This pocket of mellow beauty among the high peaks had made many as slow as the ambling clouds above.

But, as ever, not for Erdeurr and Grespuin, whose Spring of energy wilted not in the warm summer breeze.

Erduerr was cornered in a rock-gilded pool, and Grespuin's narrow eyes told of a tickle-to-be for the dark, shivering, giggling Erdeuerr.

"Now, my friend, my long bony fingers shall know of your ribs." and Grespuin advanced to Erduerr's laughs of excited anticipation.

But if Erduerr loved a good tickle, he loved more a breathless escape. Suddenly, Erduerr splashed water in Grespuin's face and slithered past to freedom. Almost. He slipped on slick carpetweed at the very portal of escape, and a delighted Grespuin was upon him.

Erduerr's high-pitched hysterics carried far and near for long, until a voice ended the play.

"Here, here is a sight, Casandia, is it not?"

The two writhing forms paused, and slowly looked up, faces patched with Summer needle.

Grespuin was the first to realize . . .

"Siniguer and Casandia! The Veem of Sereoul has arrived!" Siniguer, tall and green and smiling, leaned against a vault branch.

A buzz of yells passed the word all through the Veem of Tedrin.

Soon all rushed to greet their cousins from the South, to play, to hug.

Sereoul's Veem could be spotted among the twisting, talking, frolicking groups as darker of skin, shorter of hair; from life in a hotter Sun—life with an early Spring and a kind Winter.

Tedrin and Colia and Sereoul hugged so hard, neither could breathe.

These brothers and sister of Ganfer and Blisfur had not touched all together since the Ending of their Mother.

Tedrin and Colia jabbered excitedly with their tall, many-colored brother, Sereoul. He was Venes-like in color, but of many more seasons. Just out of their Circle, Hiola listened and waited.

All shared the sadness of those no longer with them, and the joy of seeing each other now.

Hiola's white waisthair and blue headhair stood patiently for Tedrin and Colia to finish telling Sereoul of all things. Then he spoke.

"Sereoul, is this not the perfect Circle of life for the Vuervee, ringed by peaks, the Maurians gone forever!"

"The Maurians," said Sereoul, in his high-pitched voice, which had stayed chirp-like even in his old age, "are *never* gone forever."

Hiola felt a burn of anger. Why must all say different than he, he sulked?

"Even in our land," Sereoul continued, "we have lost some to Maurian hunters. They use giant moving things to reach us. But . . . it is of much wondrous beauty here. We will drink of its love with you, knowing the berry dries if not eaten; knowing the flower will lose its petals. Knowing that all is now.

"Knowing that this loving valley," Sereoul glanced high to the peaks, "is with us until snow breaks across its guardians. And then we will return to our land of gentle, and so will the Maurians. Colia, I see not your Veem."

Hiola, unnoticed, stalked away from the group.

"My Veem, "Colia said, "must stay to harvest our Iceberries and place much fruit in frozen caves. This so we can eat through the long Winter. I came to see Tedrin—and now have found you, too."

"I admire your strength greatly," said Sereoul, "but leave you to that small Sun!"

The young of Ganfer and Blisfur laughed at this, for Colia always challenged her male brothers with her toughness. They hugged again. Tedrin had many tears in his eyes.

"I cry," he said, "because I feel this is our last valley together. Let us drink of our love, here among Summer's gentleness."

Sitting on a rock, to the far side of the Veem, Hiola stared high to the snow peaks.

I will not leave my place here for the Maurians! I belong here! My Veem will live here! The Veem of Hiola! VeemVa Hiola! Here, among these proud peaks, Hiola's Veem would carry the Circle without the Maurians. Winter cannot leave us from here. Only the frail Tedrin. The Maurians cannot find us. I will stay! My Veem will stay! Here, among these mountains I saw from my Mother's Ended form on Blue Ring. And Hiola Mented up and above them, and a true sign emerged … of a time when the grand and wild peaks would become one with him, and *all Vuervee will fly with him, proud, at last free.*

A few ridges East of his grand and wild peaks, his brother, Dillon, also waited.

* * * * * * * * * * * * * * *

"They are far away."

Young Trebel jumped from this voice behind. She turned a sharp-ened reed upon Dillon who leaned casually to a black-ened trunk.

"You sneak well," she said, strangely happy to see this blue animal.

"You stand with your mind turned within."

"I am . . . grateful for your help that night. Who is far away?"

"The Maurians."

"How can you tell?"

"The sound of Maurian boots travels many valleys. You are Maurian. For all?"

"What else could I be?"

"You have a nice face for a Maurian."

"I killed your friend."

"You wear his love around your neck."

"Grell."

"What means that word?"

"Never mind. You will tell me of your Vuervee?"

"You could not listen."

"Oh, . . . please, oh wise one, impart your sacred wisdom to this poor unseer."

Dillon had never seen a crooked smile before, and he turned his eyes from it.

"You . . . want to try that badly?" he asked.

"I'm sorry, I was being . . . sarcastic."

"Sarcause . . . "

An even, soft smile lit upon Trebel's lips. "Yes, I want to try that badly."

She was ruffled by his clear blue stare.

Dillon sat near her bundled knees. She still wore the remnants of her service tunic.

"Your headhair has much green," said Dillon.

"Only a streak."

"Have you seen it on still water of late?"

"No."

Trebel changed to sitting cross-legged. She shifted uncomfortably, feeling like she could not hide from Dillon's searching eyes and questions. His stare penetrated from innocence, she thought. From lack of motive. And then she stared at him, but her stomach fell, and she lost concentration, and . . .

She feigned a glance to the candy blue of Summer sky.

Now her face returned to his, CounterFlow etched in tart features. She was sure she had covered her unnerving awkwardness.

Dillon laughed.

"Why," he giggled, "do you make a funny face at me?"

Trebel's face reddened in anger. Freckles flared. "What do you know of anything, animal!"

"Do you know of the Circle?"

"What is this?"

"It is all of our lives."

"What is it?" Trebel asked haughtily.

"Is there much about life you understand not?"

"Yes, who doesn't? This isn't true for you?"

"Yes."

"Then what good is this circle?"

"The Circle connects the loose ends of your lines."

"You *speak* in circles. That's for sure. I have no lines."

"You make marks on a line as the day passes, yes?"

"Time. Yes, time measures the day passing."

"Here. When did 'time' begin?"

"Uncountable YearMauria's ago. Whatso?"

"All right. I give you that, yare meeri . . . "

"Just year. Say 'year,'" Trebel said, annoyed.

"Yes, year. Was there not a year before it? A 'time' before it?"

"Yes . . . well, no. I mean, it all had to start somewhere, anyso. Didn't it?"

"Then what of the 'time' just before that? A line must start at a place and End at a place, yet true life does not, nor does a Circle."

"I don't know. It's just a way of . . . "

"What of a Circle? It has no beginning and no End. Does this not tell you of all."

"That's what Duerr spoke of."

"Yes."

"So, it's a mystery. We have simply not solved it yet, though I'm sure our scientists . . ."

"And for always your friends will chase one loose end of the line, and then the other."

"So *we* are inferior, eh?"

"What means infeu . . . "

"Not as . . . far along in . . . understanding life? As a bunch of animals?"

"Yes, but we understand not the whole . . . "

"You are rude!"

"What means Reud? I am Dillon."

"Leave me alone! Go away! Instead of finding an escape from Maurian fools out here, I find an arrogant beast! An arrogant beast spewing Grell! Leave me to myself!"

Young Trebel had tears of rage streaking down her cheek. She drew her reed upon Dillon.

"Leave now, you rutted animal, before I throw these stupid buds away and have a *real* meal. I will live alone, with no one's help—least of all yours!"

She lifted the reed back to throw at Dillon, a threat in her eye. Dillon merely stared at her. Now she lowered the weapon to waist and advanced menacingly.

"Leave, I said. Leave!"

Dillon stood, gazing sky-blue from his eyes. The reed trembled at his throat. For long, his eyes searched hers. What fine eyes she had for a Maurian. An Autumn's dark green.

His stare was so deep, . . . so blue . . . her hand was frozen.

Slowly, pushing the reed back with his hand, Dillon's mouth moved at her.

The quick flash of pain from his bite sent waves of fire through her mouth, then cascaded weakness down her form.

Her legs shook.

He laughed.

Young Trebel slumped to her knees, eyes agape.

She slashed the reed at his legs.

But they were not there. He was gone. Nowhere.

A gentle wisp of Torna marked his now distant path.

Trebel fell face down, eyes closing. Her body flexed against the drug.

She cursed, why am I the one always passing out?!

And now she lay in the dreamy warmth of a Vuerven love bite. And there was a green sky, and soft blue clouds.

And there was a white Sun.

And now she was asleep, the trail of a smile turning her lip.

And she awakened not until the Sun had plunged below the snow peaks, and the night-chill sent her to her hut, which she had fashioned from branches and leaves.

The glow from the blue animal was still about her.

Next time, she vowed, she would kill him.

* * * * * * * * * * * * *

A full Moon glorified its mellow silver-gold on the colored hair of the Vuervee. When it slid to the top of the sky, all gathered in a Circle the size of a small lake, and Mented with hands held. The Moon dipped in and out behind roly, fleece-laced clouds, which became fuller and darker.

Dillon appeared from the night, and joined the Circle.

For long this Circle of Vuervee Mented.

Then all came from their trance and felt a darkening sky.

Tedrin gazed over this immense Circle of friends, clouds of sadness upon his features.

High upon a ridge, sitting on a bough, a lonely form looked down. It was Hiola, his blue and white lost in shadow, his mind separated from the Circle of Vuervee below.

Tedrin, Dillon, Colia and Sereoul passed glances among the other, though all were at far places of the Circle.

There were new faces of understanding. Muerna, Dorseurr, Windo, Trevora, Sandaleur, and Denvora had felt the soulful chill.

Young with much rusty red clung to Bobber's brown form. Duerr is.

Tedrin stood.

A breeze turned to wind. A Summer night chilled. A stand of Cuervo needle trees groaned.

Tedrin asked for the cloud pole. As the sky darkened and darkened yet, the first rumble of thunder rolled from the next basin. The Moon but suggested itself now in a vague, light thinness above. The first drops were very large, and were carried upon great gusts.

The cloud pole, breaking above the tallest trees, was raised. Atop this pole dangled and swayed the birth gem of Tedrin. Tedrin alone stood in the core of the Circle, his eyes loving around him for last.

How magnificent he was, as his arms rose through the torrent now falling. His face turned young in the filtered light. His chin thrust to the sky. Long gray-edged headhair defied moisture and waved in the storm gusts.

And then it came.

With a crack and mind-brightening flash, the flash from the clouds stunned the cloud pole, lit the rigid form of Tedrin, and the Circle of Vuervee felt it run around their ring of hands.

All saw and all remembered.

Before the energy had ceased in the tingling hands of the friends of these Veems, the Moon reappeared and the clouds rumbled on towards the Plains.

All remembered and all saw.

They saw, with clear eyes, the Ended form of Tedrin lying within them, a full red Circle in his hair, where before it was only part crescent.

All remembered the color they saw in the lightning. The color which stormed from the sky and glowed above Tedrin's peaceful face. All remembered the color was deep blue.

Dillon.

Some in the Circle said his name.

Dillon moved to the center of the Circle, standing over the Ended Tedrin.

And then all saw again:

A form burst through the outer edge of the Circle. Many remembered him to be Cirtuen, of Colia's Veem to the North.

But few have seen such sadness.

All remained still. Dillon slowly rose and walked shakily to the wild-eyed Cirtuen.

"I am Dillon."

"Dillon," wept Cirtuen.

"Tell me."

"Our Veem. Colia's . . . Veem. Ended! The Maurians, they Ended all but me. I was in the cave! They're all gone! All bleed hanging from Maurian racks, cut up and carried away as I watched my Veem drip a bloody line to Mauria. All are gone."

"The Circle is, my love," said Dillon.

Cirtuen sobbed long raking screams upon Dillon's knees. Colia wept softly.

Dillon felt the rage rise, but then his eyes softened. "The Circle is, my love. The Circle is."

* * * * * * * * * * * * * *

" . . . to be appointed within the next few days. Already plans are being made to enshrine a 46,000Book tomb for Mr. Sir Councillor Rute, surely the bravest Hero ever to take the Councillorship of Mauria.

"Mr. Sir Advisor Bordt, mastermind of the killer Vuervee capture and delivery, had this to say about his beloved leader: 'I can't . . . I can't speak my mind as to the Integrity of our great leader. He has, in death, provided a more Integritorial Mauria; both by ending the threatening cult of killers, and providing sorely needed food for all the people. For a while, and maybe forever, Grell will be a meal of the past!

"I would like to say that I . . . I appreciate the credit that's been given me for this plan, but I'd like to remind all of you that Mr. Sir Councillor Rute had as much to do with it as I did. I . . . also . . . appreciate the many inquiries asking my commitment for replacing our great lost leader; but the loss of one who trusted me totally, and whom I admired so much as our leader, has left me with no plans other than grief.

"In due of this, I am, as Acting Head of Council, assigning our great MarSek Councillor to lead a committee for selection of the new Councillor of Mauria. I am sure that Mr. Sir Dunt could not choose an unqualified Hero."

"That was Mr. Sir Bordt, Acting Advisor in Command, speaking from lN-lW. He says Mr. Sir Dunt of MarSek will supervise the selection our next Councillor. Elsewhere, Mr. Sir Bard of MarSupply now tells us that the Vuervee food is being processed at the new . . . "

Mr. Scientist Crilp tuned out the blaring box in his SonaRail.

Politics, he thought, politics and more politics! Lucky for me, I have more lofty issues than grubbing for power and slaughtered Vuervee.

And lucky he had been that WorkHouse Supervisor Steen had made the connection.

The old scientist grunted as he climbed from the parked Sona-Rail and trudged into the barren halls of the WorkHouse. As his alloy boots shuffled into the bowels of the institution, Crilp could hear sounds. Sounds of the poor souls who lived here, on the last edge of Maurian survival.

The sounds were unintelligible, but echoed a frightening despair along the corridors.

There were smells of counterseptic, sweat; wood-dry, stale atmosphere from outdated CO_2 furnaces. The first row of alloy bars appeared in buffered cross hatch. Imagine, thought Crilp, being locked in cubicles with bars for walls. He was stuck with their similarity to baby cages.

Mr. Supervisor Steen beckoned Crilp into his portico.

"You must be Mr. Scientist Crilp, I . . . noticed the young girl's name on a list from the House."

"I'm most appreciative, Sir."

"You see, she had changed her name to 'Trebel' from 'Treb.' We think she's the one that . . . made that escape a bit ago. Killed a MarSekMan. She was very . . . confused. Ran out into the wilds."

Steen handed Trebel's file and image to Crilp.

"Why," asked Crilp, "do you refer to her in the past?"

"Well, she's surely dead, . . . dead as night. No one's ever lasted . . . out there."

This one will, thought Crilp, this one will.

"I thank you for your bother, Mr. Steen, what would be a fair price for your . . ."

"Rot, Sir. I'm in no need of BookCredits. I hope the file will help you. Everso."

On the way to his SonaRail, Crilp dropped a small capsule in FareBox 27W-98N. Soon Lady Crilp would receive the last words from her dear Mr. They will say:

"To my dear Lady. I have been tended to, nourished and comforted by you. With so little left, I beg pardon for taking my remaining portion of life and throwing it to the wind. I will be past the gates of MarSek before you read this. And so I go to find her. I must see my life's work. You've served an old almost-Hero too long already. Take care. MSS Crilp. Cert UniCp."

* * * * * * * * * * * * *

The warming breezes faded each day, and now Summer opened her bright, hot tunic, and stood before all.

The long days, the calm air, the mild nights—they all seemed a permanent condition as they rolled out day after day. But it surely depended on who you were, everso, as to how you felt about this.

If you were a Vuerve, you were at peace, even as you accepted the sudden Ending of so many friends in the Veem of Colia, . . . which was no more. Isolated in this lush valley of Lola, the Vuervee lived free and unmolested. Never had they played and loved in this most secret and sacred of hidden valleys for so long! There was love, warmth, ripening apple fruits . . .

If you were a Maurian, though, the stalling breezes and the steady heat simply gave you too much time to think. Too much time to feel the heat sores in your metal boots and under your tunic.

As Winter coveted the alloy of Mauria, so did the hot beating Sun of Summer, which embraced the metal giant sprawled on the unshaded Plains, turning it into a punishing heat coil, too hot even for touch.

Too much time to gorge yourself on Prime Northern Vuervee.

You even had enough time to study the MarPrex news releases, and look for what *wasn't* being said. Because what wasn't being said— even as plates were heaped garrishly with the recently slaughtered Veem of Colia—was that CityMauria, everso, was running out of food. That four MarSek excursions into the South found no Southern Vuervee whatsoever. That CityMauria's great leaders didn't have the faintest idea where the rest of their food was living.

So, as the great oceans receded ever so slowly from this island of life; one civilization basked and lolled, another baked and sweated, . . . and an old scientist stumbled painfully up a ridge, and a small girl huddled alone in her cave.

PART FOUR:
"Autumn"
YearMauria 1241

CHAPTER TWENTY
'Ripenings'

"Put the wig on, Mauv," said Bordt, fondling a SourDrink.

"You old curse, Bordt. I'd look dumb as you in it. . . . Oh, whatso, eh? Why not give 'er a try? 'Ow many commoners even *touch* the SilverFirm Wig?"

"Silver*Form* Wig, Mauv."

"Listen to him, Mr. Sir high and grand small gamer."

Bordt grunted appreciation.

"So I couldn't break me Extract, eh?," Bordt proclaimed. "The most popular Councillor of Mauria *ever*, Mauv. Prime Vuervee on every Mr.'s table. A Hero for capturing the killer Vuervee . . . "

"You don't break yer Extract yet, Bordt. Jest 'cause yer on the FareBeam don't mean ye'll stay on it."

That was why Bordt fetched his old parlor buddy, Mauv, to serve him, be around him. His roots, his strength. With Mauv there in the SilverForm Palace at 1N-1W, he could never lose concentration—never feel out of place, over his head.

But more importantly, he could never "swell up" with himself.

She kept him in touch with the ground, the gritty truth of things. The palace, the Wig, the attention, the power—they could all make you a soft gamer if you let them.

Not with *her* around, Bordt laughed. Mauv opened the glistening Silver case and did indeed look foolish when she dropped the SilverForm Wig atop her askance and tattered features.

"Drool," she mumbled, seeing herself in the reflector. "So, ye've over gamed them all, Bordt. What next? Who's left to beat?"

"The Vuervee."

"Girl Grell! They're just animals. Anyone can game an animal."

"Tell that to Blench. He's got plenty of 10Time to listen, sitting in his quarters with no purpose the rest of his life. The Vuervee beat him. Hah! Maybe they're the ultimate foe! Too dumb for Heroism, but too smart to follow their Integrity over a cliff."

"What's all this scuff?" barked Mauv. "Jes' shoot 'em and eat 'em."

Mauv picked her teeth, then spit through her broken tooth.

Her drool landed on a stack of messages from, among others, Mr. Sir Bard of MarSupply, Mr. Sir Fruke of MarPrex, and Mr. Sir Prouse—the new head of EnvirCo.

Most of this pile had been laying there, unresponded, for many days.

Bordt guffawed breathlessly, "Hah! Yer spittle is all them high Mr. Sirs is gettin' of me! I over gamed them ruts like a hot reed through snow! Hah! Ho-de-hi!"

By 20Time later, the SourDrinks had really taken full hold. A merry Bordt and a slurred Mauv now tossed the SilverForm Wig back and forth to each other, giggling and joking. Two commoners in the highest office of the land.

* * * * * * * * * * * * * * * * * * *

Gold, blue, green and red.

How wonderful this season was, thought Trebel. After a slow lazy Sun, the crisp air of Autumn gave one a burst of breath!

She had wandered the valleys near the Vuervee. In Mauria, you couldn't really see the dark, bold blue of Autumn sky, the golding Whitebark trees, the deepening green of the needles, the fire red of carpet growth, and the red circles which freckled the ripening apple fruit trees.

Trebel crunched over fallen leaves. There was a breathless thrill in Autumn's early cool, which no Maurian but she could breathe and taste!

But a loneliness visited her for moments each day, like a shadow.

More and more, memories of Mauria haunted young Trebel. She knew she hated its gray existence, yet it was all she had to remember. There were, after all, some good things, not to be specific.

It was just that . . . she had no place to belong, to be *of*.

Often times, she would perch above the valley where the Vuervee frolicked. And watched. They seemed to be enjoying themselves immensely. Everso, as she was at the WorkHouse when a Lady visited, she felt envious, locked away, not fitting in.

And so she was lonely, being of different to all. She also thought of Dillon, and felt a strange bitterness. So much time had passed, and somehow, she thought . . . hoped that he might come after her again.

Drool, she scolded herself, you vowed to kill him! You're just lonely. The nerve of him to bite her and leave her like that! Next time, she would shove her reed through his laughing face!

Anyso, things weren't all for the Grell. She had her swimming hole, her new cave (where an underground stream lulled her to sleep each night), and her freedom.

Her freedom. Even the Vuervee didn't seem to have freedom. They were always at the will of the group.

They were just animals, anyso.

As if to remind her about the animals, a green shock of long hair swung into her eyes. While her hair had thrived untended, more bright green locks had flowered from above.

Also, her skin had darkened to a yellow-brown, freckles claiming more and more of her face. Her already thin frame had slimmed even more; so that now she was less hefty than many of the Vuervee. She wondered if all Maurians would change like this from breathing Oxygen?

But, she rarely had a view of herself and hadn't the need to consider these thoughts very often.

As now, she bounced down to her swimming hole, a tickle flirting her stomach. Today, she would pretend she was a needle cone, and the stream would carry her dancing and twisting through the smooth trough, down into the sandy pool.

And, everso, she cared not . . . but for this and the Sun.

* * * * * * * * * * * * * * * *

The SilverForm Wig regaled above Mr. Sir Councillor Bordt's jewelled ForeBar. His master tunic clung to each line of his body. He looked tall in elegant alloy boots, whose hidden risers added an imposing stature, and quelled his usually bowed gait.

"What can be done, then?" Bordt's impatient eyes darted about his advisors.

"Consumption must hold low for at least six cycles. Grell must be used," piped Helm.

"No!" Bordt snapped.

The tide of popularity he had achieved would not be threatened this soon! . . . That would be like out gaming a Hero, then losing the UniCopies!

"Mr. Sir, there's just no way of ensuring a supply if we trim the Vuervee again. Even assuming we can *find* the herd soon, figure that one adult Vuerve can feed four Maurians for a day. Add up the . . . "

"Never mind!" Bordt's icy stare aimed from advisor to advisor. "By 680Time, I'll expect all of you to have a new Heroic plan. Go and work. If an idea cannot be found, then new *advisors* can be found. Remember. Study your assumptions. Your assumptions, Heroes."

* * * * * * * * * * * * *

The frolic of swim and ray of Sun had left Trebel in a deep sleep upon her favorite rock. It lay above her sandy swimming pool. To this peaceful scene entered, hard of breath and heavy of foot, an intruder whose tube and alloy belt sent alien arcs of hard light about the soft surroundings.

Young Trebel awoke to a SonaGun aimed at her head, and an age-creased Maurian catching his breath.

Another rude surprise to wake to!

"Please. I will not harm you."

"It is typical of my people," said Trebel through a yawn, "to assure me while they aim a gun at my head."

"I am Mr. Scientist Crilp. Many years ago, I created you."

"You . . . what?" Trebel laughed in disbelief.

"You were to be my life's work. It is no mistake that you flourish among the wild. I am old now, and my only desire is to spend a few days with you. I have questions, and some answers. I was . . . almost to giving up. And I thought, I haven't felt or seen snow in so long, that I would . . . go to the peaks to die. This is quite a valley. A pocket of Summer. The Vuervee, I would guess, are just over that ridge. Quite a place. Yes."

"What kind of answers?"

"Well, for one, why you're not wearing a tube."

"Maurian bodies adjust, quite painfully. But that is all to that."

"No. Maurians all would die without their tubes, as they would without Vuervee for food. What do you eat?"

"What do I . . . whatso, look around. There's cones all the time— if you store some—and endless plants."

"Fascinating! Absolutely fascinating. You'll grant an old Hero your audience, then?"

"What do you mean, created me? And why the pride for such an accursed feat?"

Crilp looked at Trebel's freckled, bark-color face, at her dark green headhair, at her graceful legs.

"Silly young Trebel," he smiled. "You're beautiful. The perfect hybrid."

"Hybrid? What do . . . "

"You, my dear, are the one successful result of a Maurian Lady injected with Vuerven Extract."

"This cannot be! I cannot be one of those animals!"

Trebel's lips gritted protest. Her head shook in defiance.

"You are not. You are some *part* of those animals."

"So where does that leave me?!"

"Living out here, free," said Mr. Scientist Crilp.

"And . . . what of the loneliness? I fit nowhere."

"It would not be here had they allowed me to continue my work."

"That's a marvelous help *now*, old genius, isn't it?"

"It had to be done," said Crilp with a shrug.

"And what was this great need for a freak such as I am? Or you *say* I am?"

"At one time, I was very high up among Mr. Scientists."

"Well, then I must be privileged."

"You are the result of Project Hybrid. It was for streamlining Maurian form. That was the political reason for it. But my *own* hope, you see, was to develop Maurians who could live in this world—the way it *is*. Breathing, eating more than just meat. So that we could once again be independent of . . . "

"So here I am. Hah! The savior of the race I fled."

"Yes."

"I might as well kill myself now. A hopelessly unmatched mutant."

"You have your youth, which I have not. You have your health. You have these beautiful mountains and streams. Your lot is better than either world—one will be hunted to extinction, the other will watch its bellies shrink to nothing. You will live."

"*Then* what am I supposed to do? Mate with . . . oh, I'm sorry, I didn't mean that . . . "

"Please, I am a scientist. Mating does not make me ill to hear of it. You are a Hybrid, after all. Furtherso—this may surprise you—

but there was a time when Maurians Mated with each other. We die without meat now, but I'm certain there was a time . . . before we evolved ourselves away from this world . . . "

"It's just . . . what if I'm . . . the only one left?"

"It is not to that, yet. One never knows. Possibly the Vuervee will survive. At least *they* can live in the environment as it is. So can you. My plans are to talk with you some more days; and then I will be gone. When my food rations expire . . . "

"Why don't you eat *me*? Half an animal is better than none. . . . Drool, it's all a bad joke, anyso. Even before all this."

Trebel stared vacantly ahead, letting it all sink in.

She clutched to one hope—that Crilp was an insane escapee, and was making it all up.

But her heart didn't believe that.

A large tear rolled down her cheek.

"Are you . . . ," Trebel stammered, "my . . . father?"

"Life is your father," replied Crilp. "And your mother. You must believe in life."

Trebel thought, what kind of drooly old Grell is this? She started to say it, but the words dissipated, and it all crashed in on her.

She leaned forward . . . toward the scientist.

As Trebel wept gently, Mr. Scientist Crilp cradled her head. He gently stroked her green forehair, his own tear fell on hers.

A gust of wind rustled the world around them.

Autumn was gaining strength, there was change in the air.

* * * * * * * * * * * * * * * * * *

Mr. Sir Dunt fumbled at his MarSek Corder.

"Whatso?" he greeted.

"3Level MarSekMan Waurd, Mr. Sir. We've found him—got a return on his Corder. He's further West than we've ever mapped."

"Thank you, Hero."

* * * * * * * * * * * * * * * *

The Advisors gathered about Bordt, fidgeting. They radiated confidence.

"Heroes?"

"Well, Mr. Sir Councillor Bordt," chirped Mr. Advisor Quir, "we have . . . "

"Are you speaking for all?" asked Bordt, drumming his boots.

"Yes."

"It better be good. If I wanted one mind, I'd have asked one person."

"It's . . . the only solution. It is the 'core' solution."

"Whatso. What is it?"

"Sir, instead of scattering our remnantal food supply over the whole population, we *trim* the remaining herd to fully feed a sizeable minority of the people. We . . . "

"And to the others what do we say?! We seem to have misplaced your meals for the next 20YearMauria's?!"

"No, Mr. Sir Councillor. The commoners would eat a Grell of sorts. It would be made of a mix of Vuervee Grell and plant protein. Many will die, naturally, but . . . it will be just commoners, and MarPrex can conjure a disease for BlameTransfer. MarSupply will ultimately learn the minimum Grell needed for survival."

"Filler, hmmmn." Bordt was listening.

"Yes. This will allow, say, all the Mr. Sirs, many Mr.s, and a group of Ladies to eat Prime. But . . . this really just yields us some time. There's one more requisite to this plan."

"That is . . . "

"That is the beginning of a *breeding program* right here in Mauria. We will need roughly 150 Vuervee, as soon as possible. With special programs and controls, we could have a large herd after just three cycles!"

"Hmmmmn. I see. Then we have *total* control over them. Complete Integrity."

"The rest of the herd can be used for hunting."

Even Bordt's CounterFlow dropped at such a hopeful premise.

"Not bad. Not *bad*. Except the part about Grell. I'll say what: instead of 150, we shall take 300, and use only 100 for breeding. Add this to what's left of that Northern herd in Bard's MarFreeze, and we could feed commoners a one-to-three food for almost a YearMauria!"

"Excuse me, Mr. Sir Bordt, but that would really be dangerous. They're all we have left—not to mention we don't even know where the herd went, anyso. That is our last . . . "

"That will be all, Heroes," said Bordt.

* * * * * * * * * * * * * * *

Carpet growth under the tall Needle and Whitebark trees of Lola began to radiate a deep-Autumn, rusty rainbow of color. Many berries had come of season, and brightly colored Vuervee harvested throughout the valley on this cool, crisp morning. The full red apple fruits would be saved for last.

At late Sun, all Vuervee gathered for eating.

All Mented to the Winter-to-be, now that the fruits of Spring and Summer graced an Autumn feast. When the eating was done, many kinds of seeds would be carried to valley next for planting.

Of most, the mood was carefree. A day to enjoy as if all would be such. And about, many Matings basked in the cool warmth of this day, with tall piles of fruits nearby. Many a Vuerve, from another, screamed from surprise love bites, and laughed, as the dizziness and warmth caressed their forms to the soft carpet below.

Even aged Colia, determined to Ment to the sadness of all, heard Erduerr too late. The sharp pain shook her from sad Menting. Her anger carried her in winding staccato paces to meadow next, where she fell.

As she awaited Erduerr, a smile shone through her tattered soul.

Now her tall and strong form writhed beneath him, and they were a wondrous sight amidst a meadow of gold, green and brown.

Even Grespuin, searching for Sandeleur, was bitten by Casandia, who had waited above in a tree.

Many of the young played with partly mature bites that only sent them into laughing fits.

"I have to admit," commented Mr. Scientist Crilp from the peak where he and young Trebel watched, "despite my . . . scientific detachment . . . this is disgusting!"

Young Trebel giggled.

CHAPTER TWENTY-ONE
'Truth'

"Trebel!"

"Ummn, grngh, Mr. Crilp, it is the middle of the night."

"I have faulted again. The Maurians. They will come here soon."

"What are you ranting . . . how do you know?"

"What a fool! I brought my Corder here! They can track it!"

"Your . . . oh, no."

* * * * * * * * * * * * * * *

The new Sun floated upon another berry-blue sky. There was a growing crisp to the air which hinted of a Winter to come; but which was washed away in middle day.

A metal boot toed Erduerr awake.

"Ahhhhh!" and Erduerr lept to run from the Maurian. "I have not come to hurt you," said Mr. Scientist Crilp. "I have no gun. Is there a Vuerve that can speak for all?"

"H-he speaks *from* all."

"Where can I find him?"

"He is behind you, the one with all blue."

"Oh, I . . . did not hear all of you sneak up on me."

"I am Dillon."

"I am . . . Crilp. I have come to warn you."

"From what?"

"From the Maurians."

"But you *are* a Maurian."

"Yes. Well, uh, . . . I am no longer . . . of them."

"They are coming?"

"Yes. It is my fault. Their machines . . . can follow me here."

"Thank you for the warning."

"You are not . . . angry at this?"

"Your eyes say it was not planned."

"I have always . . . liked your people."

"From the size of your belly," Dillon said evenly, "I would say you have liked us much."

"I, you . . . yes. I have . . . I have eaten, of course. I have come to help you now."

"We cannot run. If they are coming, our only track from here is towards them."

"Then I may advise you?"

"Of?"

"Of negoti . . . of speaking to them. They will want to make a . . . to have an agreement."

"How can you know this?"

"I am a scientist. You are their food supply, and they are running out of food. They must work with you."

"And."

"And they cannot, so they will try to cheat you."

"This means?"

"Uh, this means to speak one way and act another. I want to be with you, to . . . speak to you about their *real* words and *real* actions."

Dillon searched this man's eyes. Now he motioned to his brother.

"Hiola. Take all Vuervee upon the bough peak, where the apple fruits ripen on the trees. Then lead all friends to the first snow peak toward the Sun from there. Crilp and I will await the Maurians in Lola. . . . Hiola, my brother."

"Yes?"

"The Veem is in your Circle while I remain here. If something happens to me, . . . you will guide them with love."

"Of the Circle, Dillon."

Now, as never, Dillon and Hiola gazed deep into each other's eyes. And, first ever, only love was seen. And sadness.

Hiola's eyes turned again to the high snow peaks which matched his own white fore and waisthair.

And his Sign told him it was there that *all Vuervee will fly with him, proud, at last free.*

Dillon said, "Hiola, you must do whatever will allow our Veem to see another Spring. If we are trapped here, . . . have them scatter all about. Some should hide, some should run. Some will escape."

Hiola nodded, his eyes still fixed on the tall, jagged ice peaks.

* * * * * * * * * * * * * * * * * * *

The Veem of Dillon gathered together, and soon the sound of all Vuervee climbing through thickets faded to the West, Hiola's staunch stride bursting at the lead.

Soon, Dillon and Crilp stood alone, with only a moaning wind to hear.

The Vuervee were gone, leaving no trace in this happy sanctuary, save for a Maurian scientist and a blue VeemVa named Dillon. And another wind sang through the cavernous walls of Lola, humming a melody against the rising cliffs.

But now, Dillon and Crilp twitched their heads to another sound. It was the grinding protest of alloy on ground carpet from the East, as the largest formation of Maurian Terrain Vehicles ever assembled rumbled into the mouth of Lola, sealing it from escape.

Dillon looked at Crilp. Now there was the blare of an amplified voice shocking the quiet valley.

"VUERVEN PEOPLE! THIS IS MR. SIR COUNCILLOR BORDT. WE MEAN NO HARM TO YOU. WE NEED TO MEET WITH YOU.

COME FORWARD. YOU ARE TRAPPED IN THIS VALLEY BY THE HIGH PEAKS. YOU MUST TALK TO US. COME FORWARD NOW. WE MEAN YOU NO HARM."

"I will accompany you," said Crilp, "so I can hear. I'll hide out of their view."

"Will they kill me?"

"I . . . no. Not just one of you, anyso. That would make no sense, whatever their plan."

Dillon and Crilp stooped under a low Whitebark and walked towards the Maurians.

* * * * * * * * * * * * * * *

The unexpected. That was Bordt's hatred of hatreds. He sensed its presence.

This valley. It didn't fit. How could there be a green, lush valley so far in the Snow peaks? This upset the confidence which had shaped his jaw over the long and bumpy ride through the night.

It was like having to game in someone else's parlor.

Yet . . . *he* had all the Terrain Pieces, *he* controlled all the squares on the board.

Anyso, the Vuervee were trapped here. They had no weapons that could pare through a line of SonaGuns.

Bordt relaxed. Here they would erect an Integritorial marker to him.

All he had to do was convince, or capture.

He had gamed the worst and the best, and had always won. Still, these creatures did have a knack for ruining plans somehow, and Bordt would not underestimate them. His creased brow reflected his concentration.

He thought of how CityMauria now revered him. If they only knew the real state of affairs—that he used the Maurian food supply as a gaming piece. But, it would be set-to this day, he felt certain.

A noise snapped him to the present.

Whatso? Only one Vuerve walked to greet the Hero of all Mauria? This blue animal worried him. Again, the unexpected. Where were the others?

"Let's move," barked Bordt, and Mr. Sir Dunt and four advisors marched eagerly behind him down a levelled patch of Torna.

As Dillon watched the small party of Maurians step down the ridge, the Sun soaked their large bodies. Their tubes glittered.

One wore long silver hair, not of his own.

Dillon remembered none of them from the last time. He felt a strange reassurance for Crilp's presence behind a tree near. Now the Maurian faces were near, and other faces flashed before him: Dragna, Brinta, others.

Ended by the Maurians.

He was frightened to feel the same . . . anger. His thoughts bounced back to him from the Maurians' cold metallic tunics. And now Bordt and Dillon looked into the other's eyes.

Dillon's water-clear stare frightened Bordt for an instant. He was not ready for such a pure, unveiled look. There were no emotions to . . . strip off, here. No fears covered by a Mr. Sir's smug disdain. Nothing to pry open that wasn't already there.

The surrender . . . how could this happen in such eyes, Bordt wondered?

But this excited him . . .

"I am Mr. Sir Bordt."

"Misserseurboard?"

"Uh, Bordt, my friend. Call me Bordt," that ending with a bemused grin to advisors.

"I am Dillon."

Bordt had never been this close to a living Vuerve before. He remained quite ill at ease.

"Do you, uh, speak for the others, uh, wherever they are?"

"I speak from them. What do you want?"

"Uh, hah, uh, well, it's quite complicated, really. I thought we could have a talk."

"We are having a talk."

"Yes, well, uh, you see . . . let me say this: You are aware, of course, that our people and yours are inter—uh, need each other."

"I'm aware of your need of us."

"Well, even at that, we must ask for favor."

"Yes."

Mr. Bordt swallowed hard. "We need many of your people. I will be honest and direct."

"To eat?"

"Eh, . . . in a way. But in the long run, you see, all your people will be free."

"How is this?"

"We plan to raise a group of you in Mauria. From this," Bordt's voice became more certain as he continued—after all, he was offering them a real chance. "From this we shall raise our own food supply. You see, this way the rest of you are free to roam and grow without threat. Perhaps some day our civilizations can then be friends. The herd will be bred for unawareness—no pain."

Bordt waited for a reaction, as Dillon's stare remained ahead, unchanging.

Now, Bordt thought, when the animal argues, I'll . . .

"I will go ask. I will find out who will leave with you," Dillon said.

Bordt couldn't repress a chortle. That was all? That simple? No gaming needed?! He was almost disappointed.

"Ah, excellent. Excellent. I knew two intelligent species could work out their differences. Oh, and, ah, we need four hundred of you; well, we'll tell you when you've brought enough. And also, ah,"—this as Dillon started to leave—"ah, it will have to be done one way, or another."

"I will ask."

"Uh, yes."

* * * * * * * * * * * * * *

Mr. Scientist Crilp puffed up to Dillon, breathing hard. His head swirled with weakness. His food rations were gone.

"You heard?" asked Dillon.

"Yes. You're not really going to ask, are you?"

"Of course. He asked me to. If there are those who desire such a life, the question seemed clear."

"Dillon, you have no choice. They will take those of you they need either way."

"This is not so, in a good world."

"Perhaps this is not such a good world?"

"The Circle is."

"I won't even *ask* about that."

"I will ask if any want to go to Mauria," and Dillon turned to go.

Mr. Scientist Crilp shrugged his whole body and plunked to a log. Dumb. How could one help these people?

* * * * * * * * * * * * * *

"Well, Dunt, not bad, eh?" Bordt massaged his own neck. "Looks like my future, and yours, is . . . in the drawer, eh?"

"Not bad, but I'll have a whatsee when they return," Dunt said, twisting dials on a SonaScope.

"Still doubt my gaming, eh?" But Bordt allowed a grin. "Have you been able to track the blue one to the rest?"

"No. He carries no alloy upon him, he is too far for viewing, we can see nothing through the growth. They must be in there, though, somewhere. Just across this valley up on that cliff, I'll lay Book. They are trapped by cliffs on all sides."

Now, a new noise.

Breaking twigs, huffing.

Mr. Scientist Crilp stumbled and wheezed from a Berrybush stand, plodding out toward the Maurians.

"Whatso! The escaped old scientist," nodded Dunt. "Shall we shoot him, Sir?

"No, "said Bordt.

Grell! Another surprise.

Bordt was suddenly tired of absorbing the growing twists and turns with everyone watching.

There was no back parlor room to retreat to, to think . . .

"I will meet the old fool up ahead."

"Sir . . . you're going . . . *alone*? I don't think that's safe, Mr. Sir Councillor.

"I've been alone all my life, Dunt," he said. Then with a sarcastic smile, "I appreciate your concern for my safety," and he fondled the Wig. "Stay here."

Bordt stepped ahead and met Crilp in view of the Maurians, but out of hearing distance.

"Will you listen, Mr. Sir Councillor?"

"Crilp, I believe."

"Yes, Mr. Sir Councillor."

Crilp's breath was labored.

"Tell me why I shouldn't shoot you this instant?"

"Sir . . . you must listen. There is . . . no way out for CityMauria on this path. Breeding will take too long, and will never be a *real* solution, anyso."

"My advisors say otherwise."

"Your advisors also have ambition."

"Not the lolly-wigged old fool they told me you were, are you?"

"Sir. You must choose your people's future over your popularity."

"What do you mean?"

"You must . . . let the scientists work on changing Mauria to a different food supply. The Vuervee are not a final answer, and only further poison Mauria's Integrity . . . independence. Everso, until we eat what is plentiful, what grows, what used to fly and crawl . . . "

Bordt stared.

Of course, there was some truth in what the old rut was saying, allowed Bordt. Everso, logic was undeniable to a gamer, no matter how disgusting the premise.

"This . . . breeding that you seek," Crilp pleaded on, "will work only for your own political good, and only for the short time. You must not let history remember you as . . . "

"That is all I need to know," Bordt said, and squeezed the lever on his SonaGun.

Crilp fell face forward into the decaying leaves of autumn.

A final puff of dust marked the scientist's last breath.

"History," Bordt whispered to the trees, "is bought and sold."

The ruler of CityMauria walked slowly back to his entourage.

"The old daff is dolly-cocked," Bordt reported. "He was going to run off and warn the Vuervee not to go with us."

But the eyes of his advisors and Dunt were looking past Bordt.

"Misserseurboard?"

Bordt jumped and spinned around, his Wig flopping over one ear.

Dillon stepped up to the Maurians.

Bordt adjusted his Wig, splashed a wide smile on his face.

"Ah, Mr. Dillon. You're very quiet. Welcome back. That certainly didn't take long."

"Thank you."

"You kill your own, also?" Dillon observed, looking back to Crilp.

"Oh, uh . . . oh, him. He was an escaped . . . criminal."

"He Ended with love," Dillon said, "I placed a Birthgem upon him, his Circle begins. He was offering you help, I heard him . . . "

"Yes. Look, Mr. Dillon, let's stay on our path, here. Well, uh, how many will, uh, enter the program? That's what's really urgent, here. Is it . . . say, as many as those trees over there, say from here to that hill?"

"Who will go with you to Mauria?"

"Yes, yes."

"None."

"Uh, aheh, none?" Mr. Sir Bordt's face turned pink.

He had been made to look a fool by this animal! Played along like the best of Gamers.

Integrity, . . . CounterFlow.

"Well, I must say, Mr. Dillon. That is bad. You knew all along that, uh, that was the case, didn't you?"

"How could I, without asking, Board?"

One advisor covered a small giggle.

Bordt dropped his mask.

"Perhaps I should make myself clearer then. *We must have 400 of your friends.* We will . . . have them one way or another. Now," a sympathetic smile, "why not choose them yourself, so we don't have to do it for you? You are trapped in this place. You can't get out. Perhaps if we reduced the number a bit?"

"I can think of no friend who will want to . . . "

"But you are trapped, animal!" Mr. Bordt's uncomprehending tendons flared through his neck-fat. "Are you not?"

"A friend of the Circle is never trapped."

Mr. Sir Bordt toed the ground.

"Grell! I've had enough of this reducement. Mr. Dunt, get your Heroes ready to move in."

"Though my friends will not go to Mate in Mauria, this does not mean we cannot come together as friends on other paths. We tire of being hunted. Let us speak of other ways. We can teach you to eat growing things from the ground, to . . . "

"Quiet, fool!"

And now a cold smile of . . . anticipation crossed Bordt's features as he ordered Dunt to summon the MarSek troup from above. A bellow of engines crashed to life as 50 SonaGates prepared to lurch forward.

"Please, friend, you will not get your way, the Circle . . . "

"Quiet, I said! You will stop these machines you see coming?"

He waved an arm behind him to the armada crunching down the hill, their wheels chewing grass and fruit. Their long, turreted guns aimed to Dillon.

Dillon looked to Bordt with ice-blue eyes.

Bordt's lip raised in a sneer of triumph as he watched the machines, gleaming metal on this Autumn day, mowing down carpet plant and Needletree in a swipe.

Dillon saw, high above, the leaves of the Whitebarks had turned bright Gold. His icy stare melted to a tear.

Bordt grinned and said, "I will let you watch."

The animal will cry! This was *better* than a Mr. Sir slumping into a chair, empty defeat in his eyes. Crying! Bordt felt an intense rush deep in his loins.

This would be the best one yet.

Then Dillon turned, lifting arms to the sky, blue headhair waiving; and signaled to Hiola.

Perhaps, Dillon thought, some will escape.

* * * * * * * * * * * * * * * * * *

The Vuervee shivered atop an ice-cliff crowned with last Winter's unmelted snow. The Veem of Dillon and those of Sereoul stared to the valley below, and to Hiola.

Apart, Colia kneeled and stared at Hiola, her rugged form frowning in thought.

Now, Hiola saw Dillon's waving arms, and knew he was to tell the Vuervee to scatter, to hide, to run—that a few may escape through the Maurians.

Yet he did not tell the Vuervee to do this.

Hiola was angry.

So! . . . once again we crawl and let the Maurians poison our Circle! Now the hunters push us from this most perfect of all valleys.

The Maurians, Dillon had said, wanted to Mate us in their metal city. Our mountains, streams, sunsets, . . . all for the Maurians, while we huddle in their city of tangled lines.

Once again, Hiola started to tell the Veem to climb down and scatter, . . . and once again, he could not.

He closed his eyes tightly, letting the Sun filter through his lids and lashes. Images pulsed by—steam, a noise, a scene from the floor of a womb, . . . tiny eyes, newborn eyes . . . a flash of metal . . . a form, . . . sucking noises, a shiny tube on a large, wide man . . . a Maurian? Another form, high above . . . his Mother? Blisfur? . . . crying . . . more noise, then steam.

The Vuervee stared quietly at Hiola, a sea of eyes in a sea of colors.

Hiola Mented more deeply.

Tall, white peaks . . . his color . . . deep blue sky . . . one large cloud in a Circle shape.

Hiola opened his eyes.

He looked up.

There was a deep blue sky, and there was one large cloud formed in the same Circle he was shown.

And then he remembered . . .

* * * * * * * * * * * * * * *

Bordt rode atop the largest SonaGate, chortling to Dunt. "Ho-de-hi, Dunt, that's the last I waste talking to those fools, by the time . . . ."

"Sir, look!"

"What, . . . what is it?

Bordt snapped up to see whatso . . .

"No," he said, "oh, no."

Even the lumbering SonaGates stopped, almost as one.

Some of the MarSekMen climbed above their SonaGates, and watched with unblinking eyes.

Mr. Sir Bordt's face froze in a smile of numbness.

Dunt squinted a little, and one lip covered the other.

Across the Valley of Lola, against the white backdrop of snow, a glittering rainbow of colors twinkled before sailing down toward the rocky gorge under the ice cliff.

This red and green and blue and yellow rain of Vuervee shrieked as one, from leap to flight with hands holding feet, in a soaring Circle.

Down, down, down, they glided, fell, sailed.

In the center of this plunging Circle, Hiola screamed, " . . . *and all Vuervee will fly, proud, free at last!*"

As this Circle that was the Veem of Dillon reached its rocky womb, each Vuerve crashed into the growing heap of already broken and Ended Vuervee.

Then there was quiet.

And then one last form perched on the snow ledge.

Colia.

As she leaped, Colia screamed, her words echoing about the valley of Lola, "Dillon must live! The Circle is!"

And then, "Ah-oughng!" as her form broke near her friends.

And then quiet, again.

Not even a wind could be heard.

And then, "Have we, did we . . . did we kill all the . . . all the Vuervee from the other raid? Uh, did we . . . you know, up North?"

But no Hero was listening to Mr. Sir Councillor Bordt.

Instead, they wore a variety of mad grins and empty eyes, as the final truth sank in.

A wry grin settled upon Bordt.

He wondered how *his* eyes looked, as the purpose and strength drained, leaving the helpless surrender he so often sought to see in his own victims.

He wished he could see *his* eyes.

You can't game someone who is willing to lose it all, flittered through his head. But it mattered not now, anyso.

Around and about, some of the Maurians began to cry.

Others used reeds on themselves, not willing to starve slowly.

Still others grouped around and spoke of odd plans to save all. "We'll take the bodies, and, uh, you know, get Extract from them, and, uh, breed them anyway. That'll work, won't it? Won't it?"

There was one Maurian who wavered not, who cried not.

It was Mr. Sir Dunt.

He removed the SilverForm Wig from Bordt's head. Bordt just stared.

"CityMauria will not end with the wig atop a small gamer."

Dunt carefully smoothed the wig, ceremoniously placing it on his own head.

He spit into Bordt's face, but it didn't change the latter's mad grin.

Mr. Sir Dunt opened his Corder.

"Heroes of MarSek, " he blared. "This is Mr. . . . Sir Councillor Dunt. We have all done our Heroic mission and now we shall return home. To Mauria. With Integrity. You who kill yourselves, you who whine and scream and cry, are no better than these animals. Home, Heroes, Home."

But no other SonaGate followed the clank of Mr. Sir Dunt's as it left Lola, away from the setting Sun.

* * * * * * * * * * * * *

Dillon had climbed the ice-cliff.

Colia's scream rung in his ear.

No! Dillon must *die*—not live—before the pain of all friends Ending came over him. As he climbed on a partly frozen bluff, he saw the Earth, on this day.

He sat, to look for last at a flaming sunset, a Circle of light ringing the snow peak. He stared at a chute of Coyotia, which struggled through the snow and rock, reaching for the endless home of the sky.

He looked at his hands. The last Vuerven hands on Earth. He would End now. He would join the Circle of the Veem of Tedrin, the Veem of Colia, the Veem of Sereoul, the Veem of Dillon.

Forever to End, to begin again, forever. He would leap now.

He rose toward the edge of the cliff.

Before he could fully reach his feet, another's hand held him down.

He turned to young Trebel, who offered him a large, dew-spotted apple fruit.

He bit of its sweetness, not knowing why, as he stared into her deep green eyes. Dillon began to weep, and his head fell into her lap. Young Trebel stroked his hair. Her eyes cradled his blue forehair, misted in her own wind-blown green locks, then she stared over the peaks.

And over these peaks, past CityMauria, even beyond the Plains; the ocean tide withdrew further from a rocky beach; and a small round snail crawled up the sand, heading for the trees.

At the top of valley next, at Blue Ring, a Circle of Mindo plants was tarnished with the red and gold of Autumn. The plants bent with a full burden of winged seeds, ready to break their pods, and fly.

Blisfur is.

And by a warm spring, near the collapsed remnants of a twig-thatched womb, a rusted metal tube stood guard over a steam-shrouded pool.

Kurk is.

The Circle is.

THE END

PRINCIPAL VUERVEN CHARACTERS

GANFER (VeemVa) and BLISFUR Mated, producing her first brood:

    TEDRIN: Son

    COLIA: Daughter

    SEREOUL: Son

BLISFUR succeeded GANFER as VeemVa upon his death.

Later, she Mated with KURK (Maurian), producing her younger brood of Maurian/Vuerven hybrids:

    DILLON: Son

    HIOLA: Son

    VENES: Son

After the death of BLISFUR; TEDRIN, SEREOUL and COLIA separated, forming three different Veems. DILLON, HIOLA and VENES remain with their half-brother and VeemVa, TEDRIN.

PRINCIPAL MAURIAN CHARACTERS

KURK: (Mr.) 14th ViceCouncillor of MarPrex, Mauria's Populous Relations

BLENCH: (Mr. Sir Councillor) Head of Control Council, Leader of all Mauria

GRANES: (Mr.) Middle level Mr. of LifeCo, Mauria's science and reproduction

BORDT: (CommonerMale), small gamer, independent parlor owner

FRUKE: (Mr. Sir) Head of MarPrex, Populous Relations

RUTE: (Mr. Engineer) Head of EnvirCo, Mauria's engineering

TREBEL: (CommonerFemale) WorkHouse and cleaning girl

BARD: (Mr. Sir) Head of MarSupply, Mauria's food and processing

DUNT: (Mr. Sir) Head of MarSek, Mauria's military and security force

BURN: (Mr. Sir) Head of LifeCo, reproduction

CRILP: (Mr. Scientist) Retired. Hybrid experimenter

POWER STRUCTURE OF MAURIA

Councillor of Mauria   (Office of the SilverForm Wig)

MR. SIR COUNCILLOR BLENCH   (Chairman of Control Council)

                           (Councillor of Family Industries)

Control Council	(Governing Body)	
Family Industries	(Conglomerate)	
LifeCo	(Reproduction)	MR. SIR BURN
MarPrex	(Populous Relations, media)	MR. SIR FRUKE
MarSupply	(Food & Drink Distribution)	MR. SIR BARD
MarSek	(Military, Security, Hunting)	MR. SIR DUNT
EnvirCo	(Engineering Sciences)	MR. ENGINEER RUTE

ABOUT THE AUTHOR

 **STEVE NORTH's** versatile career includes writing science fiction stories and writing and producing over thirty national televisions shows with his wife Barb. His published science fiction short stories include "The Sweetwater Effect" and "Days of Present Past." He has written and produced for such television shows as *Fantasy, Make Me Laugh, Candid Camera, The Gong Show, Anything for Money, Totally Hidden Video*, and many more.

North has also written numerous documentary films for Coronet and Britannica Films, as well as two feature films, *Burger Wars* and *Letting Go*, both penned with his wife and optioned by Hollywood studios. He has appeared on numerous daytime and evening talk shows, and he has been profiled in the *Wall Street Journal, Wired* and the *Los Angeles Times*.

Steve North lives with his wife Barb in Woodland Hills, California. *Mauria* is his first novel and was primarily written in the mountains of Colorado.

9 780983 126171